BLAIR DENHOLM
SHOT TO THE HEART

By Blair Denholm

The Fighting Detective

Fighting Dirty
Kill Shot
Shot Clock
Trick Shot
Shot to the Heart
Drop Shot
Point Blank
Moving Target
Cold Shot

This one's for a wonderful friend. Uwe Detlef Rinke, you left this world too soon, but you enriched the lives of many. See you on the other side one day, champ.

Vinci Books

vinci-books.com

Published by Vinci Books Ltd in 2026

1

Copyright © Blair Denholm 2022

The author has asserted their moral right to be identified as the author of this work in accordance with the Copyright, Designs and Patents Act 1988. This work is a work of fiction. Names, characters, places and incidents are the product of the author's imagination or are used fictitiously. Any resemblance to actual persons, living or dead, places and incidents is entirely coincidental.

All rights reserved. No part of this publication may be copied, reproduced, distributed, stored in any retrieval system, or transmitted in any form or by any means, including photocopying, recording, or other electronic or mechanical methods, nor used as a source for any form of machine learning including AI datasets, without the prior written permission of the publisher.

The publisher and the author have made every effort to obtain permissions for any third party material used in this book and to comply with copyright law. Any queries in this respect should be brought to the attention of the publisher and any omissions will be corrected in future editions.

A CIP catalogue record for this book is available from the British Library.
Paperback ISBN: 9781036708269

The EU GPSR authorised representative is Logos Europe, 9 rue Nicolas Poussion, 17000 La Rochelle, France
contact@logoseurope.eu

Prologue

MCNAIR'S BOXING Club lay in wait at the end of the alley like a vengeful enemy. It was the club where Jack Lisbon trained and fought as a young man. It still bore the name of its original owner and founder, Angus McNair, a light-heavyweight who abandoned the tough shipyards of Glasgow to pursue a boxing career in London.

The tale of the rise and fall of Angus McNair was the stuff of urban folklore. Jack had heard the story a hundred times, often with different endings, depending on who was telling it. Some elements were undeniable truths. Others were shrouded in speculation.

As Jack and his daughter Skye strode down the alley, hands gripped together, his mind harked back to the colourful history of the gym and its eponymous owner.

Angus McNair, apprentice welder with a guaranteed future of drudgery had he remained on the docks, had a special ability. He could fight like a tiger. After moving to London, he rapidly climbed to the top of the light-heavyweight rankings. A rare talent, he defeated every opponent who stood in his way. McNair claimed the title of British Southern Area Champion in 1968 by conquering the legendary West Indian pugilist, Clive Anderson. Killer Clive, loved and respected as a hard-but-fair boxer, had made the fateful error of not retiring in time. Cocky to the point of arrogance, 41-year-old Anderson agreed to defend his title by taking on the younger, fitter, hungrier Angus McNair. By the accounts of those who attended, it was a classic duel, a dog fight that went the full fifteen rounds. The canvas became so slippery with blood, sweat and spit that the boxers, slipping and sliding, had to expend massive energy reserves just to keep their feet. The champ Anderson fought bravely, with every fibre of his being, taking innumerable blows to the head and body. He hit the canvas twice, clambered to his feet and shaped up to resume the battle both times. As the surviving footage shows, he dished out as good as he got, also sending McNair to the deck two times. At the final bell, the referee raised the Scotsman's hand, new champion by a split decision.

Over the next two years, Angus McNair grew in skill and mental toughness, defeating every contender who dared step into the ring, the majority by knockout. He scraped together enough money to put a deposit down on a loan to buy the derelict R.J. Grace boot factory in Peckham, South London. Over the next year he converted it into a rudimentary gym, setting up a future for himself and his young family.

He hired a manager to run the gym and concentrated on his boxing career, dreaming of making the big time in America, his name in lights at Caesar's Palace. But, just like Anderson and a thousand fighters before him, McNair came to believe in his own invincibility, fought one fight too many when he should have hung up the gloves. That was one version of the story of the fall of Angus McNair, and a plausible one at that.

According to the second version, McNair's trainer, renowned disciplinarian "Sugar" Richard Higgins, pushed his charge into the bout when he hadn't fully recovered from a bad shoulder injury. Again, it wasn't too hard to agree with that.

And then there was the third version, the one aired in bars and lounge rooms around London to this day. The one Jack believed.

The man who took down McNair was a dirty southpaw from the East End, Alexander Gallagher. One balmy summer's night in 1973, in a crowded, smoky auditorium in central London, Alex Gallagher shattered Angus McNair's dream of retaining his title for a record sixth time. He also shattered the plucky Scot's jaw, nose and cheekbone. Gallagher sat McNair on his backside ten seconds into round eight with a savage combination of head shots. Fifteen minutes later, the Scotsman was in the back of an ambulance, struggling to breathe through a smashed nose, a mouth turned to pulp, blocked with twisted cartilage, broken teeth, swollen lips and tongue. Two days later Angus McNair died on a hospital bed. Internal bleeding leading to heart failure.

How had the fight taken such a lethal turn?

According to the story Jack believed, between the seventh and eight rounds of the fight, Alex Gallagher cheated. He'd run out of ideas, McNair was dominating, closing in for the kill. Surrounded by his trainer, cornerman and cutman, who obscured the view of the referee and any cameras that happened to be filming, underneath his padded boxing mitts Gallagher slipped on a pair of weighted gloves. They were made of light material and had pockets filled with flat bits of steel. These made his punches three times harder and heavier. The assertions could never be proven, especially with the passage of time, yet Jack had no doubt about its veracity. Why? Because in his formative years Jack had come to know Alex Gallagher well, after the man had become Jack's own mentor in the junior ranks. And he'd learned the boxer-turned-trainer was an unethical, unscrupulous, contemptible bastard.

A decade after the deadly bout, Alex Gallagher secretly purchased the gym from McNair's widow. Where he got the money from was a mystery then, and a mystery today. In a gesture of magnanimity, Gallagher bestowed upon it the name of the man whose life he'd taken in the ring. Gallagher successfully maintained the pretence he was only the manager of the gym, that it was owned by a secret syndicate. But after his death five years ago, it was revealed the deeds to the boxing club were in Gallagher's name. Why he chose to hide his ownership remained a mystery, one Jack, despite his natural curiosity, was in no way keen to unravel. *Let buried dogs lie, sunshine.*

Chapter One

ON A COOL AND CLOUDY AFTERNOON, Jack stood in a cobblestoned back alley in South London, clutching a tiny hand, contemplating his next move. A paraphrased Clash tune came to mind. *Should they stay or should they go?* Should he lead his daughter away from this place of bad memories, or should he let her learn about the reality of his past? The smart thing would be to leave – take her to the zoo, to the London Eye for a spin, maybe Madam Tussauds or a cruise up the Thames. Something fun that a girl her age would enjoy.

Then again, why shelter her? She was a tough kid. She deserved to know more about her own father, about his roots. And for that to happen, a visit to McNair's Boxing Club was mandatory. Besides, Skye herself said she was dead keen to check the place out. She'd seen most of the famous attractions the capital had to offer, but never the inside of a grimy South London gym. And Jack would protect her. What could go wrong?

The blinking neon sign out the front had been fixed

since Jack's last bloody visit five years ago. And a new door had been installed, solid steel with a security number pad. Back in the day, anyone could simply walk in off the street, pay the entry fee, do a spot of training and be on their way. The gym was a democratic facility, accessible to all. Gallagher was happy to take anyone's money. But lately things in the old town were changing, and not for the better. Jack had read a newspaper story about a spike in street crime in recent months, even a random terrorist attack less than a mile from where they stood. An extremist of some faith or other hacked a grandmother to death with a machete in broad daylight. Now it seemed even a gym full of tough geezers was scared. Which went some way to explain the new security arrangements.

Jack cupped an ear to the door. Faint sounds of activity inside. A humming blended with intermittent clanks. The new door must be inches thick, he couldn't tell if there was one person inside training or a hundred. He knocked hard and waited for half a minute. No response. He gazed down to his left. 'You sure you want to go in there, love? It's nothing special, you know. Just a gym.'

'Yes, I'm sure. I want to see where you learned how to be a boxer so you could collar all the villains and toe-rags.'

Jack raised an eyebrow. 'Where did you learn to speak like that?'

'Watching cop shows on television.' He'd have to have a word with his ex Sarah about the girl's viewing habits.

He knocked two more times. No luck.

Maybe it's not meant to be after all. With an apologetic shrug, he tugged Skye's hand and turned to head back to the other end of the alley, when a track-suited youth with a spring in his step stopped, removed his headphones and smiled at Jack, then Skye. Garbled rap music escaped the cans. 'You need help?'

'We'd like to go inside for a look.'

'Why?'

'I used to box out of this gym when I was a lad. My name's Jack Lisbon.'

The lad's eyes widened, as if the name meant something. 'One second.' He turned, tapped a combination of eight numbers, which Jack discretely observed and memorised. The door made a beeping sound and the teenager shouldered it, held it open with his back and waved the visitors in. 'After you, Mr Lisbon and guest.'

Then, a hesitation. The question repeated in Jack's head. *Should they go in or not?* Surely what happened five years ago was fading in people's memories. Alex Gallagher's murder made national headlines at the time. Jack prayed that half a decade later the matter was no longer a topic of conversation.

'You two comin' in or what?' said the lad, tapping a foot.

Jack clapped his hands and exhaled heavily. 'Yeah, why not!'

The wiry youth disappeared behind a rack of disc weights and Jack and Skye stood blinking in the dimly lit open space. Besides the refurbished entrance via the alleyway, not much had changed since Jack was last here, when he'd emptied the safe of tens of thousands of pounds and legged it from the scene of the gruesome crime he'd committed. He took in the same old boxing ring with its tattered turnbuckles, the same old concrete floor, cracked paint on the walls, ancient body building equipment. Off to one side, the small administration area, home to filing cabinets full of personal records, and also the place where Jack had killed Gallagher with a sharp letter opener to the jugular. How he itched to get in there, see if there were any blood stains left behind after all this time. Overarching everything tangible was that characteristic smell, almost a taste, caressing the palate of his mouth. A blend of chalk, liniment and stale sweat. To Jack that aroma was like the finest perfume.

'As I live and breathe.' A voice came from behind his left shoulder. Jack turned to see a familiar face, a man roughly his own height and build, lighter coloured hair and features that were much less battered. He dabbed sweat from his underarms with a fluffy white towel. 'It's Jack Lisbon, back from Oz. And who's this?' The man looked down at the beaming young girl gripping Jack's hand.

'All right, Bruiser.' He could hear his own London accent, softened after years in Australia, thicken as he spoke to another born-and-bred Cockney, Lex "Bruiser" Buskin. Jack gazed down at his daughter, his chest swelling with pride. 'This is my girl, Skye. I thought I'd show her around the old stomping ground.'

'Not a nice place for a young lady, though, is it?' Bruiser shook his head. As Jack recalled, the man was a stock market trader who liked to spar with semi-professional boxers. He was almost good enough to have a crack at competitive boxing himself, but the man treasured his good looks too much to risk it.

Jack pointed at two ripped, pig-tailed women sparring in the ring in the centre of the gym's floor. One was almost blue with tattoos, the other a clean skin. The sound of leather smacking hard against exposed flesh echoed in the vast space. 'What's that all about then?'

'They're older,' Bruiser retorted. 'They've been around

long enough to make the dumb decision that it's OK to beat the femininity out of each other.'

'Equality, Bruiser. We're not living in the old days any more, are we?'

'True enough. Oi, listen. We've all been keeping an eye on your exploits in Australia. All over the telly you was, in the papers too. You've made a name for yourself, that's for sure. Solving crimes. You even foiled a bank robbery single-handed, dincha?'

Jack felt his face flush as Bruiser laid it on thick.

'Daddy's the most famous policeman in the world. No bad guys can get away from him.' Clearly the embarrassment cooking him from the inside out wasn't shared by Skye. Which only made things worse.

He bent down to the level of her face. 'Come on, sweetie. Enough of that. I'm trying to keep a low profile here.'

'What's that mean?'

'It means,' laughed Bruiser. 'Your dad here would rather no one paid him too much attention. Makes him feel…'

'Awkward.' Jack finished the sentence for him. 'I'm on holidays, the less fuss and bother the better.'

'Sure, Daddy, whatever,' said Skye. 'Can I go watch the ladies fighting?' Her eyes were as big as the medicine balls lining the walls.

There was too much enthusiasm in Skye's request for Jack's liking. On the other hand, a close up view of the pain the women were inflicting on each other might act as a deterrent. 'Sure.'

'Oi, Detective Lisbon.' A nasally, annoying tone. *Does every conversation here have to start with Oi?* A man with ropey sinews made his way over to the visitors, a swagger in his step, undoing white wrist wraps as he went. In his peripherals, Jack had seen him emerge from the shower block area, the light of recognition flickered in the man's narrow eyes. He quickly clocked Jack and Jack clocked him. Patrick "Paddy" Sheehan. Some of the abundant scars on the approaching man's face were gifts of damage inflicted by the late Alex Gallagher in an act of inhuman savagery. Jack could scarcely credit the man hadn't given up boxing after what happened to him.

'Paddy.' Jack nodded. 'Still brawling I see.'

'Yeah. I recovered enough after…you know…the incident, to make a comeback. I compete in a couple of fights a year.' An awkward laugh. 'Nothing to get excited about, but it helps pay the bills, know what I mean?'

'Yeah.' Jack was glad he didn't have to eke out a living like Sheehan. Jack had a day job back in Australia that paid well, offered security, a pension plan and all kinds of other perks. Fighting to make ends meet when you weren't that talented a pugilist meant Sheehan must be desperate for cash. 'Winning many?'

'Ha! Since I dropped down to flyweight, I'm cleaning up.'

Jack assessed the almost anorexic body. His opponents must be junkies even worse off than him if he was beating them.

'Great. I'm glad. Now, if you'll excuse us, we're off to watch the ladies spar.'

A hand darted out and grabbed Jack by the wrist. 'Any chance of a word, guv?'

'Sure, what's up?'

'In private.'

'You can tell me in front of the kid.'

Sheehan shook his head. 'Please.' He gestured to a wooden bench next to a groaning weight rack.

'Skye.' Jack took a couple of pound coins from his pocket, dropped them in her palm. 'Here, go buy yourself a Coke or something. Then you can watch the girls in the ring. Don't stand close, but. The minute you're out of my line of sight, excursion's over and we go home. Understood?'

'Yes.'

'Good.'

'You know you can trust me, Daddy. I'm ten now.'

'It's not you I don't trust. It's everyone else.'

She raced to the vending machine, waited for the plastic bottle to drop, scooped it up and skipped over to watch the women in the ring. The punching had slowed, much to Jack's satisfaction. The women were winding down, the sparring would end shortly and Skye would get bored and come back to her dad. He turned to a fidgety Sheehan. 'Now, what is it you're so keen to tell me?'

Chapter Two

'IT MIGHT HAVE BEEN a bad idea for you to come back to England, guv. Something doesn't feel right. People are looking for you. People we haven't seen around here before.'

'Leave off, Paddy.' He'd known he was walking into a potential danger zone, but World War III wouldn't have stopped Jack coming home to Skye. 'I'm perfectly capable of taking care of myself. And my daughter.' Jack held up his dukes and mock snarled. Sheehan didn't flinch. Then a quick glance to make sure Skye was where she was supposed to be. She was. Perhaps a little too close to the edge of the boxing ring, but out of harm's way.

'I'm serious. I'd be real careful if I was you.'

'Don't be daft. You've taken too many blows to the head.'

Sheehan snorted under his breath. 'I might look like a weedy runt, but I'm fitter and faster than ever. No one can lay a hand on me these days. Which means no concussion and my thought processes are like a bleedin' computer.'

'Yeah, a toy one, maybe. So, who are these dangerous people looking for me?'

Sheehan edged closer. The invasion of Jack's personal space required a hand to the shoulder and a shove away to restore a comfortable degree of separation. 'Sorry, guv,' Sheehan apologised meekly.

'Keep your poxy, sweaty mug away from me. I'd be more than happy to reacquaint you with Mr Concussion if you're interested.'

'I said I was sorry! Geez, you ain't changed much, 'ave yer?'

'I haven't got all day, sunshine. I'm already sick of this shit-hole.' He waved a hand at nothing in particular. 'I'd like to take Skye for a burger and a movie before Sarah's curfew kicks in…' Jack consulted his wristwatch '…in about three and a half hours. So unless you've got anything specific to tell me instead of vague warnings, I'm not interested in gossip.' Despite the dismissive tone, uneasiness gripped Jack's stomach. He'd made sure to leave no traces when he killed Gallagher. The police investigation had fizzled out, the case was filed away in the archives as unsolved. The fact Gallagher was a scum bag definitely helped Jack's cause. The Met would always prioritise hunting down killers of the truly innocent ahead of killers of low-lifes who had it coming. And yet…could someone in the police have Jack in their sights? Anything was possible. A zealous detective with something to prove, digging around in the cold cases, could uncover something initially missed. Or someone else who actually gave a shit about Gallagher seeking revenge?

'I know you done it,' said Sheehan, the words soft as the beating of a butterfly's wings.

Jack's heart stopped for a moment, his mouth instantly dry. *Calm down, Lisbon.* 'What did you just say?'

'Micky Knox told me everything. How he was there that night when you…'

'I did nothing,' Jack hissed through gritted teeth that failed to stop a droplet of spittle launching from his mouth. 'Knox was lying to you.'

Sheehan's sly grin made Jack sick in his gut. Why the hell had he come to McNair's today? Ironically, Jack understood, the decision had turned out to be a fortunate one. He already knew he'd have to be on his guard. Now he was on high alert. 'Hmm,' Sheehan continued through pursed lips. 'Micky seemed pretty convincing. But don't worry, guv.' A tap to the side of his bent nose. 'Your secret's safe with me.' A trio of noisy youths with fancy razor-cut hairdos walked in front of the two men. Sheehan dropped his voice to a faint whisper. 'You did the world a favour getting rid of that prick. After what he done to me, I'm forever in your debt, guv.'

'Micky's talking out of his arse. I'm no murderer.' Lying came too easily. 'But I ain't surprised people might think I am. It was no secret there was no love lost between me and Gallagher.'

'Yeah. Plus you had that big confrontation with Gallagher the day before he was killed. How you dusted off them younger lads.'

'That's common knowledge. It was all investigated and I was cleared of everything. Nothing to associate me with the murder.'

'Micky reckoned you could've beaten ten men that night. Like the bleedin' Incredible Hulk. He told me all about how you sat a couple of blokes from Gallagher's stable on their backsides, right over there.' Sheehan pointed at the glass partition to the office. 'One of them still trains here regularly, believe it or not. Elrod Smart, the black lad you knocked out.'

'That's also in the public domain. Smart tried to fit me up for assault but the charges were rightly dismissed out of hand. I was defending myself from a gang attack!' Jack paused, took a deep breath. 'All that shit came out in the investigation.'

'Did the bit about you taking the money from Gallagher's safe come out in the investigation too?'

'What the…?'

'I told you, Micky opened up to me. He told me how you peeled off some banknotes for him. I know everything.'

Jack ignored the remark, switched tack to the most pressing agenda item. 'So, enough stalling. Who's looking for me?'

'A big beefy Scottish bloke, McTaggart I think the name was. Eat's a shit load of porridge judging by the size of him.'

'Who the hell's he? Name's not familiar to me.'

'Me neither. He wandered in off the street the day after you arrived in town.' Sheehan gently chewed a ragged fingernail, spat out a severed sliver onto the floor. Jack cringed but offered no reproach for the gross act.

'How did he *wander in off the street* as you put it? What about the new security panel?'

Sheehan shrugged. 'Someone must've let him in. Just like they let you in, I guess.'

'You've gotten smarter over the years. I can barely credit it,' Jack chuckled.

'Any road, this McTaggart hung around for a bit, did some sparring with one of the lads, Johnny Hannan it was. Johnny was outgunned and the Scot gave him a boxing lesson. When he was done, he asked a few blokes if they knew your address, me and Micky included.'

'What did you tell him?'

'Nothing, guv. No one knows where you're staying.'

'What about my old address? Or Sarah's?' Jack heard tension creep into his voice. The mashup of gym sounds faded to nothing as he concentrated on Sheehan's words.

'Nobody remembers that stuff, guv.' Sheehan wriggled in his seat. 'You've been away for five years, or is it six, I can't remember. Besides, the bloke never enquired about your ex.'

'So where's this McTaggart now then?'

Sheehan shook his head. 'He disappeared. Hasn't been back since that one visit. Maybe there's nothing to it, after all.' The man's tone of voice brightened slightly. 'He coulda just been a geezer who heard about you in the news and knew you had an affiliation with McNair's. Wanted to meet the famous Jack Lisbon, innit?'

The notion that a fan of Jack's exploits would go to such an effort was flattering, but it seemed unlikely. 'I don't think so, Paddy. Your initial instinct is right. Something smells and I don't like it. I didn't exactly advertise the fact I was back in town.'

'You know the gossip mills in these parts. Only takes the whisper of a rumour before the cat's out of the bag. Perhaps your ex said something to someone she shouldn't have at the beauty salon about you coming home. She's still working at that place on Blenheim Grove, ain't she? My Maisy used to go there, reckoned that Sarah was a wiz in the fingernail department.'

Jack shook his head. 'No. She moved to another beautician's near the Denmark Hill tube station end of last year. Had a falling out with her old boss, apparently. Not surprised, really, she's a bloody temperamental woman. Sarah, I mean, not the old boss."

'Don't matter which one she's working at. Those parlours are the perfect place to set tongues wagging. Women sitting under hairdryers for hours at a stretch with nothing better to do than talk. Then they tell their pals on Facebook 'n that. It's almost impossible to keep your business private these days without taking extreme bleedin' measures.'

This time a slow, knowing nod from Jack. 'You're rather insightful for a man who resembles an anorexic weasel.'

Sheehan ignored the comment. 'After that, it's a domino effect, innit?' He crept closer to Jack on the bench, a steely glare enough to stop Sheehan's advance. 'So, let's assume word of the great detective's return did get out. Maybe the mysterious Scotsman was sent by someone to do a bit of digging.'

'Yeah, but who?'

'Someone in Gallagher's family,' Sheehan ventured hopefully. 'One of the brothers, his children, maybe his widow wanting revenge.'

Jack rubbed a hand across his moist brow. 'Jesus Christ, revenge for what? I didn't fucking do anything!'

Sheehan laid a hand on Jack's wrist. 'Steady on, guv. I bleedin' told you I'd keep the secret and I meant it. I'm not the prosecutor here.'

He was right. *Ease off, relax.* Jack stared into space for a few moments, thought about the people Sheehan had mentioned. He knew the details well. He'd been involved in the investigation into Gallagher's murder, questioned, harassed and threatened. Many in the force suspected Jack, he had motive and opportunity, but his denial skills worked as well as any combination punch he'd ever unleashed.

Plausible deniability. *Deny, deny, deny*. The lead investigator, DI Chris Dreyfus, had harried him like a terrier, but to no avail. Besides, there was no incriminating physical evidence. Jack had disposed of the weapon and cleaned up after himself better than TV serial killer, Dexter. Most importantly of all, there were no witnesses other than Micky Knox, who's role in the cover-up and acceptance of money made him an accomplice and therefore guaranteed his silence. Or so Jack had thought. He prayed Sheehan was the only person Knox had told and that's as far as it went. At the end of the day, though, Jack had gotten away with it. Once ensconced in Australia, he'd followed the case via online news reports until it petered out. But he hadn't been able to fully switch off, and he never would. Now here he was, back in the danger zone.

Time for a quick mental recap. The details of the main players in Gallagher's life were etched firmly in Jack's brain. Pamela Gallagher, the trophy wife 20 years younger than her husband. A Swedish-born one-time model who fell in love with Gallagher's money. Word on the street, she scored the bulk of her dead husband's estate and promptly left Britain. Why would *she* want revenge? The very idea was nonsensical. Indeed, she'd been a prime suspect at the beginning, under the microscope, but there was nothing to pin a contract murder on her. Gallagher's other beneficiaries were two grown-up children, Cedric and Alicia. Residing in the counties of Shropshire and Suffolk respectively, both were said to hate their father for his boorishness, probably a little less now dad was six foot underground. A pair of hypocrites, they'd enjoyed the fruits of their father's criminal activities by receiving the best education money can buy in the United Kingdom. Cedric was an architect and a shire councillor, Alicia a successful dentist with her own practice. They, too, had been cleared. If they knew Jack had offed pop, surely they'd be grateful rather than filled with thoughts of vengeance.

Then there were the twin brothers, Charles "Chopper" and Simon "Slasher" Gallagher. Today they lived together in a rundown council estate in Fulham, wallowing in their poverty, surviving on government welfare. Their nicknames were bestowed on them ironically by brother Alex when they were kids. Jack remembered Gallagher telling him about his weak siblings. It was over 25 years ago but so vivid in Jack's mind it could have been yesterday. *'A pair of useless no-hopers, my brothers. No fucking ambition. You ain't gonna be like them are you, young man?'* Jack said no way, he was going to be a world champion boxer. At the time he was convinced of it. He adored trainer Gallagher at the beginning of their relationship. Love became toleration, then dislike, finally – hate.

Jack fished a packet of extra-strong chewing gum from his jacket pocket, tossed a handful of pellets into his mouth, mashed with vigour to get the flavour hit. He turned back to Sheehan. 'I can't imagine any of them caring about what happened to Alex Gallagher. His widow buggered off to Milan with an Italian gigolo, his children despised him and his brothers never gave too hoots about him neither. If they knew I'd…taken care of him, they'd only be glad.'

'It's a mystery then.'

'Or maybe it's nothing other than your fertile Irish imagination.'

Their conversation was interrupted by a small girl with a sad frown. 'Daddy.'

'Yes?'

'I don't wanna watch fighting any more.'

'Not for you?'

A sharp head shake. 'Nope. I thought I'd like it, but it's horrible. Can we go now?'

Jack scanned the gym, saw the tattooed woman hobbling towards the dressing rooms, clutching at her stomach and blood dripping from her nose. So much for the idea the women had been winding down.

'Sure, sweetie. Let's go see that movie I promised you.'

Chapter Three

THE SUN SHONE brightly through a maze of chem trails from the hundreds of jet planes zooming in and out of London each day. But the British sun was a different beast to the Australian one. It illuminated a lot better than it warmed. As if to emphasise that fact, a cool breeze wafted across the grassy meadow. It ruffled Jack's hair, half an inch longer since the last visit to his Yorkville barber five weeks ago. Back were the beginnings of his natural yet unfamiliar waves. Life as a copper in stinking hot North Queensland was a lot easier with a short hairdo. The shorter the better. It felt liberating now, not having to worry about maintaining his military-style cut to impress colleagues or frighten villains. Skye would take him no matter what he looked like, he knew that instinctively. A drop of melting chocolate icecream landed in the new spiky beard covering his chin. He dabbed at the blob with a small white napkin, ran a hand over his whiskers. Sticky. Perhaps the emergent holiday beard needed a rethink.

On a bench by a walking path in a sprawling South

London park, known by locals as The Common, Skye snuggled in against his side. The feeling was like nothing on Earth. Before the move overseas, Jack would have rated his performance as a father as pathetic. He'd not exactly neglected her, but he'd not devoted the time she deserved. Still, her love for him was pure and unconditional. Perhaps the old adage was true, and absence really did make the heart grow fonder. Whatever the case, the urge to protect and to nurture his child almost overwhelmed him. He'd missed her so much over the past five years. Leaving her was going to tear his heart in two. Then a thought.

'Hey, kiddo.'

'What?' She looked up at him, melted chocolate rimming her lips.

'How would you like to come and stay with me for a while?'

Her eyes lit up. 'At the Airbnb place you're renting in East Dulwich?'

'No, silly. In Australia.'

The transformation from seated child to one leaping up and down on the spot was so quick Jack barely registered it. 'Yes, yes, yes!' Droplets of thawed ice-cream sprayed in all directions, including on Jack's trousers.

'Hey, hey, calm down. I've got to run the proposal past your mum first. So don't go getting your hopes up.' He immediately chided himself. Her mother would never agree.

'She does say some nasty things about you, but if I beg hard enough she might say yes.' It was as much hopeful question as statement.

'Does she often give in to your begging?'

The excitement faded as fast as it began. She sat, took a forlorn lick of her ice-cream and sighed. 'No. She's a big meanie.'

'Really?'

'Uh huh.'

'She let you come out with me today, didn't she? And we don't have to be back until much later.'

'Yeah.'

'Then she can't be that tough on you, can she?'

Another sigh. The kid was good at them. 'I guess not. But,' the voice dropped to a conspiratorial whisper, unnecessary in the open air with no one within earshot, 'she's organised a shopping outing with her girlfriend Ramona from the new salon she works at. They both took the day off. It was kind of convenient you taking me off her hands for the day.'

'Surely she doesn't think of you as an inconvenience?'

'No, that's a 'zaggeration. She—'

The whistling flute intro of Men at Work's "Down Under" interrupted the discussion of Sarah's parenting abilities. He'd switched the "London Calling" ringtone soon after the plane touched down at Heathrow. Using that cliched tune here would be like taking coals to Newcastle, Jack had reasoned, thereby creating a geographical dog's breakfast of a comparison in his mind. He pulled the phone out, hung up without looking at the number and stashed the device back in his pants pocket. This was his day with his daughter and he wouldn't be interrupted.

'What's that movie you wanted to see again?'

'Again? I haven't seen it for the first time.' She grinned, knowing she'd caught him out smartly.

'You know what I mean, don't be cheeky.' He was suddenly bursting with pride for the daughter he'd missed for years. A kid with a quick wit would have the edge later in life, in a world where you had to stay one step ahead of the competition. He could take no credit for it; either mum was her inspiration or it was a pure natural talent.

'It's the new Spiderman one.'

'How many of them have there been, for goodness sake? I'd say at least twenty.'

'I think only eight, Dad. One for each spider leg,' Skye giggled.

A quick scroll of the Samsung Galaxy and a raised eyebrow from Jack. 'Wow. Damn close, sweetheart. Mr Google says it's nine films in the franchise so far. But…oh no, don't tell me…they're planning even more.'

'Come on, Detective.' She grabbed his wrist and tugged. 'If we don't hurry up they'll already be on the movie set making the next one.'

Chapter Four

AS THEY GOT up to head for the bus stop at the edge of the park for the connector to the Cineworld complex in Wandsworth, Jack realised he was grinning like an idiot. He couldn't care less. He had his beautiful and, more importantly, *smart* daughter holding his right hand and life was a bowl of cherries.

A raucous burst of flute from his jacket pocket stopped them in their tracks. 'I should've left this thing back at the flat.'

'That's the second time, Daddy. Why don't you just take the call? I don't mind. It could be important. Maybe Inspector Batista needs your advice on a case.'

The kid had boned up on all Jack's famous cases from online press reports, knew the names of all his colleagues in Yorkville like they were family. 'Very well.' He ripped the phone from his pocket, pressed a button to reduce the volume as he eyeballed the screen. Number withheld. After his conspiratorial conversation with Paddy Sheehan, a phone call with an unrecognised number on this device set his heart thumping again. He scanned the area to check there were no suspicious characters lurking about. The coast seemed to be clear. But who could this be harassing him? He recalled there were two SIMs nestled inside his new Samsung: one his Australian number if, as Skye correctly surmised, Yorkville CIB needed to contact him about something, the other – his reactivated old London number. This call had come through on the latter and no one had rung him on it in five years. The only person he'd expect to hear from on the local number was Sarah. *Must be effing spam.* He pressed the red cancel button, pocketed the phone. He resolved to create a separate ringtone for the Aussie number so he could distinguish the two without having to look at the screen. Perhaps it was time to resurrect The Clash.

'Why'd you hang up? Was it Mum?'

'Ah, no. Probably someone trying to sell me aluminium cladding or something.'

'What's that?'

'A kind of roof guttering.'

'Don't you live on the first floor of an apartment block in Australia? You don't have a roof, do you?'

Before Jack could respond to Skye's accurate description of his housing situation, the insistently annoying "Down Under" rang out again. Nothing for it, curiosity won over. He jabbed a forefinger at the green button. Out of the corner of his eye he saw Skye squint and tilt her head to the right, eavesdropping without shame.

'Yeah, wot?'

A scratchy voice spat out the words, 'Hey, Jack. It's me.'

A London accent, and clearly not a friendly salesman. The identity of the voice's owner couldn't be ascertained based on that scant introduction. Further enquiry was needed.

'Who are you?' Jack barked. 'I'm a very busy man.'

'*Look out!*' someone yelled from behind Jack and to his left. An errant frisbee, spinning viciously, homed in on his nose. Instincts developed over a lifetime of brawling kicked in. He dropped his hands to his sides, arched his back and swayed out of the way, as if evading a hostile fist. The aerodynamics of a rotating frisbee in a park on a gusty day, however, differ radically from the trajectory of an assailant's fist. In other words, its route can only be guessed at. Jack guessed wrong. The orange disc followed Jack like an Exocet missile, clipped his earlobe before crashing into the trunk of an oak tree.

'Fuck me!' His hand shot to the wounded ear, cupped over the throbbing flesh.

'Language, Daddy. There are children around.' Skye pointed at a group of toddlers in a portable plastic playpen, eyes agog as the strange man hopped up and down.

Jack gently palpated his earlobe, scanned forefinger and thumb. He brandished his palm, two red droplets glistened. 'Taking you out on a date is dangerous, madam. Look at all this blood.' Despite the mild stinging sensation, Jack couldn't suppress a smile. The repeated '*ello, 'ello* emanating from the mobile at the end of his arm reminded him someone was still keen for a chat.

'Sorry, I was just attacked by a UFO. Now, who the hell is this?' Jack waved away the approaching woman who carried the offending toy and wore a guilty smirk. Must have been the one who chucked it. She didn't get the hint, put her hands on her hips and offered a pursed-lip smile. Clearly waiting for an opportunity to say sorry, but Jack wasn't interested. He tucked the phone under his chin. 'It's

OK, love. Just a flesh wound. Think I'll live. Now, if you don't mind.' He gestured for her to leave with a flick of the hand. Relief washed over her sweaty face, she mouthed "thanks" and walked away.

'It's Micky Knox.' The voice was 60-grit sandpaper on gravel.

The little bastard had some nerve calling after spilling his guts to Sheehan. 'How did you get my number, Knox? I don't recall ever giving it to you.'

'I went back to McNair's after…you know…the incident.'

'You what?' Jack couldn't believe his ears. The man must have had balls the size of watermelons to return to the bloody crime scene.

'Yeah. I dunno, I thought maybe you'd missed something worth pinching after you'd offed Gallagher.'

The skin on the back of Jack's neck prickled as Knox calmly spoke about the crime Jack had committed, with his innocent daughter standing not six feet away.

'Anyway,' Knox continued. 'I stumbled on Alex Gallagher's little black book with all his contacts in it and I took it. Thought it might come in handy one day. And guess what? It has.'

'Enough, Micky. What do you want?' It was a struggle to stay calm, but he had to. Skye was listening hard. No need to alarm the wee tyke.

'Look, I'm calling from a payphone and I ain't got too many coins, so I shan't be long.'

Payphone. That explained the lack of a number being displayed. It didn't explain what the rat Knox wanted.

'I won't interrupt. Talk.'

'There's a big Scots heavy looking for you, I–'

'I'm well aware of that. You spoiling my day to relay old information?'

'Thought you said you weren't gonna interrupt.'

'Sorry.' Staying quiet was going to test all Jack's resolve. As far as Jack recalled, Knox was a lad whose primary loyalty was to himself.

'Just let me get it all out. Then you can make up your own mind. Wait, I'm feeding my last two coins in.' *Clunk, clunk.*

For the next three minutes Knox's words sent a shiver down Jack's spine. It was all rumour, but still, the possible repercussions... The lad freely admitted to telling Sheehan about the night Jack had killed Alex Gallagher with a letter-opener to the jugular, how Knox himself had profited from his role when Jack peeled him off five grand from the stash stolen from Gallagher's safe. *Why did he blab?* Knox felt Sheehan needed to know his own brutal bashing for throwing a fight had been avenged. Sheehan swore the secret would stop with him and Knox believed he'd stuck to his word.

But, independent of this, there were whispers spreading all over London that Jack had come back to gloat. To show the world he'd gotten away with murder and wasn't afraid to show his face again. The investigation may have cleared Jack, but the court of public opinion was still divided, with many believing the version that Jack was the killer. And then Knox's narrative shifted gear and got real interesting. 'I reckon I've got a minute left.' His raspy rapid speech only added to Jack's anxiety. 'Here's the thing. There's rumours that Gallagher's kids didn't despise him as much as he led everyone to believe. He wanted to act the tough man, appear as if he cared about nobody. Some folks reckon the offspring never hated him as a person, just the way he earned his money. It was daddy who put them through college and gave them the best start in life. In other words, they're convinced you offed their pappy and now they want blood.'

Jack's hand darted to his ear, suddenly throbbing. 'They're hardly fear inspiring. A dentist and a...what's the other one?'

'An architect. But that one, the son, he's also in politics. A councillor in Shropshire. Which means influence. So, I just wanted to give you a heads up. Be extra careful, orright? It could all be unfounded. Still, that big Scottish bloke turning up seems a bit too coincidental. No one's been asking about you for ages, now these rumours start flying about.'

'Thanks, Micky. One question though. Why are you so concerned about my wellbeing all of a sudden, huh?'

'You done right by me, guv. That money you gave me paid for some online courses that set me up nicely. IT for small business. I started a consultancy, do all right for myself. Do a bit of drop-shipping 'n that.'

Before Jack could ask why Knox was shipping drops or dropping ships or whatever the hell it was, a woman's blood curdling scream sent the lunchtime park visitors into a frenzy.

Chapter Five

THE PHONE VIBRATED in the depths of his pants pocket. It could only be one person. His one-off paymaster. 'Have you got him in your sights?'

'Yeah. I followed him to the park. Him and the kid. I've got a direct line of sight.' About 50 metres from Jack and Skye Lisbon, the observer sat cross-legged on a bench. The remnants of a roll-up cigarette dangled from the fingers of his free hand. Dressed in black jeans and a dark grey hoodie, top pulled over his head, the lad felt lines of sweat trickle behind his ears. Flower beds lay between him and his surveillance subjects, but they were low enough to allow a clear enough view. Every now and then the observer stood, paced back and forth as he spoke on the phone, waved his free hand in a chopping motion. The aim was to portray a person preoccupied with a phone call and not at all interested in his surroundings.

'Has he got any idea he's being watched?'

'I can't tell you what's going on in his head, but I'm guessing no.'

'Excellent. What are they doing now?'

'Nothing exciting, just sitting there.' The observer paused, shot a glance towards the subjects under surveillance. He took a last hungry draw on the ciggie, crushed it with a twist under his shoe. 'A minute ago Lisbon bought himself and his daughter ice-creams.'

'What else?'

'Nothing else. Just the two of 'em enjoying a day out. Boring stuff.'

'Don't be cheeky, son. I'm not paying you to be cheeky. I'm paying you to be observant. And accurate. Remember you said you were only too willing to help because you hate Lisbon, correct?'

'Yeah.'

'That's all well and good, but I need more than motivation, I need you to pay attention, all right?'

'OK, I got it.' The job was paying a lousy 100 quid. The prospect of getting back at Jack Lisbon was a persuading factor, however the threat of a beating by the big Scotsman if he refused was the real clincher. That aside, he did relish the thought of the bastard copper suffering. 'He bought the ice-creams from a mobile kiosk. They're sitting on a bench eating them and having a laugh. He's wearing a pale yellow polo top, tan chinos and blue-and-white trainers. Asics. I can tell from back here 'cos I got a pair just like 'em. He probably hasn't changed much compared to the photos you would've seen online, articles about his career in Australia 'n that. Only difference, he's got a bit of salt-and-pepper stubble going on and the hair's about half an inch longer. He looks fitter than most of the younger people hanging about the park, lemme tell you. Muscles popping out of that shirt. The kid's in blue jeans and a white spray jacket. Pink trainers. Got a great shock of curly hair on her. Cute as a button.'

'Very good, son. You're proving you've got an eye for detail.' A pause, the sound of seagulls squawking in the background. 'Can you tell if he's carrying?'

'He's got a Harrods shopping bag, if that's what you mean.'

'No, no, no. I mean does he have a weapon on him, for fuck's sake!'

'Oh, that.' The man must watch too many American movies. 'It's hard to tell from back here.'

'Then use that compact set of binoculars I told you to buy. I hope you kept the receipt. I like to keep my accounts tidy.'

'I don't have them.'

'Why not?'

'The store you sent me to was out of stock and it was too short notice to order them in. I tried a few other places, no good.'

'Never mind. Can your mobile phone's camera zoom in?'

'Dunno, never tried.'

'Give it a go. Most of 'em you just expand the image with your thumb and forefinger, know what I mean?'

'Yeah, give me second.' He fumbled about with the mobile, terrified he'd lose the call and anger the man. He spread his fingers on the screen and the targets doubled in size. He couldn't expand indefinitely without the image going blurry. 'From what I can see, there's no bulges in his clothes, so he probably doesn't have a gun tucked under his belt or whatever. But I can't be totally sure.'

'I'm gonna assume he doesn't have one. Unlikely there'd be a pistol sitting in the bottom of a shopping bag. The bloke's an ex-fighter, a pretty good one they say, so I guess he normally ends arguments with his fists.'

'Yeah, prob'ly.' The observer was getting bored listening to the guy. He just wanted the operation to be over so he could get the hell away from here, back home, to the pub, anywhere.

'There's no CCTV in the area is there?'

A quick glance around 'Not that I can tell.'

'There's over 600,000 of the bastards in the city of London and they're always putting in new ones, so you can't be too careful. I've traced the location of your phone…'

What the?

'…and matched it with the map of known cameras in the park, and you seem to be in a section free of them. Lots of trees and grass. I'm assuming my map's accurate, but I don't trust the powers-that-be to be completely upfront with their citizens, know what I mean?'

'Yeah.' He lit another cigarette, cast his eyes around for another sweep of cameras. Maybe they were disguised as lights up those lampposts? Or in the trees?

'Based on the evidence, I'm going to assume you're in a CCTV blind spot.' A blowing sound, like the bloke was trying to cool down a cup of hot tea. Then a slurp. 'What about their mood, how are they behaving? Tell me what you've noticed since you started tailing him.'

The observer started to yawn but suppressed it. No need to piss the bloke off unnecessarily. Nobody wants broken kneecaps for an early Easter present. 'Right, I've seen a proud father taking his daughter to the park for some refreshments before they head off to the movies.'

'You sure your intelligence is accurate on that?'

'It's what I've been told. Doesn't matter but, does it?

Your bloke said you'd be carrying out the operation here in the park.'

'True. But I'm the type of person who needs to know everything. I'm anal like that. If something goes tits up, I want you to keep following him, see what he gets up to, regroup. We've got options. Always have options, sonny. That's my life motto. But nothing will go wrong, I can feel it in my waters. Please continue.'

'Fine. I've noticed Lisbon's been clinging on to the kid's hand at every opportunity like he doesn't want to ever let go. He looks at her with this weird expression, kinda like a first-time father would stare at his new-born baby.' Gilding the lily, but the bloke was lapping up the details.

'That's better, son.' The voice was thick with condescension. 'Lisbon's got skin in the game, as they say. More likely to do anything for her, which makes him vulnerable.'

Whatever. 'OK, Now the kid's jumping up and down all excited. Lisbon musta promised her a flippin' pony or something!'

'Ha ha. I like your humour.'

He likes my humour but he'll break my legs if I don't do as he says. Fucking psychopath. And all I get is a lousy 100 quid.

A few moments passed in silence.

'Hey, you still there?' said the man.

'Course I am. Nothing's happening, innit? Oh, wait, he's on his mobile. Turning his head so the kid doesn't listen in, I reckon. Seems whoever's on the other end of the line is doing all the talking. Lisbon's face is moving all over the place. He's real concerned about something.'

'So he should be.' An evil chuckle on the other end of the line sent a shiver down the observer's spine. 'I wonder who he's talking to?'

'I'm too far away to eavesdrop on his call, so I can't

answer that one.' It was only then that the penny dropped. *Lisbon's got skin in the game.* 'Hey, you ain't gonna do anything to the kid are you? You said no one was going to get hurt.'

'Relax. As long as Lisbon doesn't do anything stupid, no one *will* get hurt.'

The assurance sounded hollow.

'Holy shit!'

'What?'

'They just got up to go when a fucking frisbee's collected Lisbon in the head. Unbelievable!'

'Excellent.'

'What?'

'All part of the plan. I wanted to shake him up, throw him off balance before we strike. What's happening now?'

'A woman's coming over, he's waving her away. She's backing off. He's ended the phone call and he and the kid seem to be making a move to leave the park. What now?'

'Like I said, wait around in case there's a problem.'

'Gotcha.'

Precisely eleven seconds later all hell broke loose. The sudden scream was the loudest the observer had ever heard in his life, frightened him so much he dropped his mobile on the ground. He picked it up to continue the conversation, but the call was disconnected. There was no way to ring back, he didn't know the man's number. A thudding noise was getting louder and louder. Jack Lisbon was sprinting along the pathway, waving his hands about and yelling *Get out of the way! Police! Don't move!*

The observer averted his gaze as the detective sped past, but then shifted his eyes to Lisbon's back, arms and legs pumping like pistons. Lisbon reached a woman, surrounded by a crowd of about a dozen people. She sat cross-legged on the ground, shoulders heaving. Lisbon bent down to comfort her. A choked-off muffled sound coming from the opposite direction made him twist his head back around. In the confusion created a hundred metres from where Jack and his daughter had been sitting, a very large man had made his move. He had one arm wrapped around Skye's waist and the other around her mouth. The observer expected to see her wriggling, kicking hard in protest. Instead, she was limp as a rag doll.

And then, she was gone.

Chapter Six

A LONG CAREER as a law enforcement officer had ingrained something fundamental in Jack Lisbon's brain. When you hear a cry for help, you react. Fast. 'Someone's in trouble. Stay here and don't move. Do you hear me? I'll be right back.'

'I take the bus to school on my own every day, Dad. I think I'll be OK.'

'You sure?' Probably best she stayed put. Who knew what danger lurked where that awful scream had some from?

'Of course I'm sure. That poor woman needs your help.' Skye constructed a concerned face with her bottom lip pointing down and her brow furrowed, as if her own mother was in dire peril. 'Go on. I'll be fine right here.'

Jack stood, felt the muscles in his upper thigh flex as he prepared to run. He'd managed a light jog this morning to get the body back into shape. Jet lag was still working its evil magic, but after two days his system was almost back to normal. Two strides in and he realised he should've concentrated on stretching as much as the morning jog itself – his hamstrings were taut fit to pop. Jack hadn't run this hard for months. Twenty strides in, his body involuntarily twisted at the waist so he could check on the kid. Still on the bench, kicking her feet back and forth, smiling and waving. All good. *That girl is so proud of me it hurts.*

He passed a youth slouching on a bench, not caring too much to lend a hand. Bloody self-centred adolescents these days. Too busy gawking at the screen of his phone to care about a fellow citizen. *Where's your sense of civic duty?* He'd be sure to have a word with the lad once he'd sorted out the problem.

Only a couple of strides away now, the woman who screamed was obscured from view by the assembled crowd. A hubbub mingled with the woman's jerky sobbing. Jack slowed to a jog, sucked in the big ones to get his breath back. He shouldered his way between two middle-aged women with frightful perms. The people encircling the victim took a step back. The law had arrived. Jack's emphatic 'GET OUT OF THE WAY, PLEASE!' helped matters along.

To Jack's astonishment, the woman on the ground was the frisbee thrower who'd nicked his earlobe a few minutes earlier. Mousey-brown straight hair tied back to reveal a high, intelligent forehead. Not a trace of make-up on a perfect complexion. A trim body clad in high-waisted khaki shorts and a white tank top emblazoned with a Nike swoosh logo, toned arms and legs. Her freckled face was flushed, cheeks damp with tears.

'What happened?' Never beat around the bush when there's a crowd of rubberneckers surrounding you.

'She was attacked by a...' came a timid male voice from behind Jack's left shoulder.

Jack spun around. 'I was asking the lady,' he snarled at the do-gooder, easy to do since the man closely resembled a maths teacher Jack had hated at school. The bystander was cursed with a nose upturned to such an angle the nostrils were almost perpendicular to his face. Amazingly, beside him stood a drop-dead gorgeous redhead, her arm linked through the crook of his elbow, head leaning on his shoulder. The man must have charms beyond the physical.

'Sorry, I just wanted to...ah...'

Jack ignored the man, dropped to one knee and gazed into the victim's green eyes. 'Are you OK, love?'

'Y-y-yes.' She reached across and grabbed Jack by the collar, pulled him so close he could smell the sweet odour of peppermint on her breath, as if she'd recently brushed her teeth. 'I was attacked by a man who stole my purse,' she whispered. 'Oh my, it happened so fast. It was all a blur. I was heading for the park café to get something to eat when someone tapped me on the shoulder. I turned around and this bloke shoved me in the chest with both hands. Before I knew it I was flat on my back, he'd grabbed my purse and taken off...' she pointed a shaky finger towards a gravel path leading into a densely wooded area '...that way.'

'Describe him, quick as you can.'

'Hmmm, lemme think.' She dabbed at her eyes with a tissue. 'I'd say he was about your height. Red baseball cap with a Manchester United logo, dark glasses, black t-shirt with some kind of rock band picture on it. Arctic Monkeys, that was it. Tatty jeans. Oh, and an ugly piercing like cows have in their noses. He was on the chubby side, so if you hurry you might catch him.'

'Gottcha.' Jack stood, dusted blades of grass off his

chinos. He addressed the small crowd, now comprising about fifteen people. 'Has anyone called the police?'

'I thought you *were* the police?' said the man who spoke first, his screwed up eyes enhancing his porcine appearance. 'You yelled it out as you were running over here.'

'Yeah, I am 'n all, sunshine. Just not my jurisdiction. Make yourself useful, get on the blower and call 999.' Jack inhaled deeply and took off on his third run of the day.

———

'DID you see a fat man running through here? Red hat?' Jack puffed at a woman in a shell tracksuit coming in the opposite direction pushing a pram, eyes glued to her phone. A startled head shake. Turning a bend, Jack almost collided with a teenage couple holding hands and staring into each other's eyes. He repeated the inquiry, another negative response. A further minute into the chase, two more sets of shrugged shoulders, and alarm bells started ringing in Jack's head. *Something's off about this.*

Then, his priorities shifted gear. Skye! Why did he leave her there on her own? *Think rationally, Lisbon.* There were dozens of people in the park today. Nothing could happen to her in public like this, in broad daylight. But something *had* happened to the frisbee lady, hadn't it? Or…? Oh, sweet Jesus. She said everything happened in a blur, but was able to describe the mugger in such detail. Right down to the Man U cap and the t-shirt. *You idiot, Lisbon!*

He hared off down the track, pushing himself even harder than on the outward leg. He estimated three minutes or so separated the alleged robbery incident and now. Pig-nose and his wife, at least Jack presumed it was his wife, were the only ones left at the scene.

'Where's the damn victim?' Jack snapped.

The woman let go of her man and took a step forwards. 'We volunteered to wait around for you, and this is the thanks we get. You've not got very nice manners, have you?'

'What?' Talk about touchy.

'I've not forgotten how you were rude to my darling Roger. I dare you to be rude to a lady. Go on, I dare you.'

'Look, I'm very sorry.' Jack shielded his eyes from the midday sun, glinting off the glass of the orchid conservatory and laser-targeting his retina. A spark ignited in his chest, set off a raging fire that coursed through his neck and face. He nodded understandingly at the redhead. 'Right, let me try again. WHERE. IS. THAT. WOMAN?!'

Jack's burst of ire had zero impact on Ginger. 'Gone,' came the deadpan reply.

'What? Where?' A passing cloud stopped the glare off the glasshouse for a moment. Jack scanned the bench he and Skye had been sitting on. It wasn't empty, but that brought no joy. It was occupied by a trio of strangers. *Jesus, where is she?*

'C'mon Roger, let's go home,' said the woman.

Jack raised a hand to stop the pair from leaving. 'You two aren't going anywhere. Stay here until I get back.'

'You can't order us about, you aren't a local copper, you admitted it,' said Roger, suddenly brave after his woman had stood her ground.

'Maybe not, but I know plenty, and a few who owe me favours. Right now, I don't care what happened to that woman. Did you see a little girl?' Jack described Skye like he was giving evidence in court, not a detail missed.

Roger ran a palm over his chin. 'No. Did you Faith?'

She shook her head. 'Nah. Who is she?'

'My daughter.' Jack had an idea. On his phone he

pulled up the photo of Skye he took this morning standing outside Sarah's apartment block, held it out to the couple.

'Oh, very pretty,' said Faith.

'A real cutie,' said Roger.

Their words triggered a horror scenario for Jack. It would be bad enough if she'd been snatched by people wanting to get to him, but there was another, sicker, breed of abductor out there. A child like Skye alone in a park could prove irresistible to the wrong kind of creep. *Shit.*

'You go look for her,' said Faith. 'We'll wait here to answer any more questions you wanna ask. OK?'

Jack forced a smile. He'd been too harsh on them. 'One more thing. Did you call the police like I asked?'

'No. Not long after you took off, the woman stood up and said not to worry. It was just her boyfriend she'd argued with and she made up the bit about an attack. The other people lost interest and wandered off. We stayed behind to let you know what happened.'

'What the hell…Was she delirious?'

'No,' said Faith. 'She regained her composure quick smart. Stood up and wandered off like nothing had happened. Calm as a cucumber.'

'I think you mean cool, dear,' said Roger, brows lowered.

'Look,' said Jack. 'Could you please call the emergency number?'

'And tell them what?' asked Roger, his tone eager, face animated. High drama in the park must be the ultimate in excitement for a dullard like him.

'A woman was attacked and the assailant's on the loose. Ask them to send some officers ASAP.'

'But she said she'd made it up,' said Faith. 'Won't we be wasting the police's time?'

'That's not your concern. I'll deal with it. The whole episode smells and I'm not liking the odour. Please do as I say. If my daughter's missing because I got sent on a wild goose chase, that bitch is going to wish she'd never been effing born!'

Faith held up a finger like she'd had a light-bulb moment. 'Why don't you call the police yourself? It's your kid after all. And you said you had contacts there and–'

'I've got my reasons,' Jack interrupted. 'Actually, I think you're right. I'll take care of that.' Then, his own light-bulb moment. He wouldn't call the cops. Not yet. He conjured a benevolent smile for Faith. 'In the meantime, perhaps you could ask around, see if anyone's seen my daughter, OK?' Jack entered her mobile number on his Samsung, sent her an MMS message with the photo of Skye. *Bing*, message received. The couple nodded and set off purposefully to quiz the public.

Adrenalin was giving Jack serious palpitations, but he had to relax. A cool head was needed in a crisis, he knew from experience. Five years ago he'd defused a bank robbery single handed and saved the lives of dozens of people. Unarmed and unafraid. The same recipe could be required again today. He was up to the task, all he had to do was focus.

Jack rushed to the people now occupying the bench. *Their bench. His and Skye's bench.* His heart beat like a trip hammer, if he didn't rein it in he'd collapse or have a heart attack. *Calm down, son. You don't know anything yet.* She's probably had an urgent call of nature and gone looking for a toilet or somewhere in the bushes to pee unobtrusively. Like she said, she travelled to school on her own now. She wasn't a baby. His eyes darted from what appeared to be the father to the mother to the snot-nosed son, then back again. He quickly introduced himself, showed them the photograph of Skye.

'Didn't see no one,' said the female. 'When we got here the seat was free, so we took it.'

'Yeah', confirmed the adult male. 'Little George here's all tuckered out.' He wrapped an arm around his child, pulled him close. 'We've walked miles and he finally couldn't take another step, poor little fella.'

'Are you sure you didn't see her? Look again.'

'Yes, we're sure,' said the woman. 'With all that gorgeous hair, how could anyone miss her?'

As he'd done with Roger and Faith, Jack enlisted the help of the small family. 'No problem,' said the man. 'We panic if we lose visual contact with George even for an instant, so I get you, pal.'

'Meet me back here in thirty minutes, or earlier if you find Skye.'

'Understood.'

Jack fired off an SMS to Roger and Faith with the same instructions. He headed for the wooded area, eyes alert for any clues. Two adolescent males en route said they hadn't seen her. Another twenty minutes went by in a flash. He got negative reply after negative reply from whomever he questioned. Almost time to meet the others back at the bench.

As he marched back to the meeting spot, a though stopped him in his tracks. If Skye was missing because someone wanted to get to Jack, he might need some serious assistance at the top level.

He scrolled through the contacts on his London SIM and found an old acquaintance he hoped was still working in the London Met. Detective Chief Inspector Lars Pedersen worked in the Specialist Crime Command and had one of the best clean-up rates in the UK. Pedersen was also one of the few officers who remained friends after Jack departed the Met five years ago under a cloud. They kept in semi-regular touch via emails, although their last contact was over a year ago. Jack went to press the button when a message preview appeared that made him sick to the stomach.

Chapter Seven

THE BURLY MAN pushed the ice-cream cart along a winding stretch of path by the narrow river. Mallard ducks quacked merrily, white swans glided along without a care, the happy shouts of children playing carried across from the other side of the river. The man whistled unmelodically, like people whistle when they're guilty of something but want to appear innocent. He'd seen this trick on TV, usually accompanied by back-and forth eye rolls, a ruse so obvious it drew attention to the fact a person actually *was* up to no good. He wouldn't roll his eyes and give the game away. He wasn't stupid. Just whistle nonchalantly and push the jaunty red-and-white cart. Out the exit and into the waiting white van. Another couple of minutes and he'd be there.

A middle-aged woman in a beige raincoat smiled warmly at him as he approached. She looked like his Aunt Mabel. She tossed some breadcrumbs from a paper bag, attracting raucous ducks like a magnet. He raised the little white hat he'd pilfered from the vendor to add a touch of authenticity, offered her a friendly "how d'you do". There'd been no time to take the rest of his uniform, but it would've been pointless. The bloke was about three sizes too small. But the hat was all he needed to become the Ice-cream Man. The woman smiled again, all gums, gave a friendly wave before throwing more breadcrumbs into the water.

He'd been fully prepared to take the kid in the semi-open, depending on how well the diversion went. Apply to the face a handkerchief soaked in a homemade chloroform mix, then a sleeper hold, quickly drag the semi-conscious victim into the bushes, gag her with gaffer tape before wrapping her in a full-length puffer jacket complete with hood, and carry the sleeping kid to the van. It was a longish distance, but he'd done enough commando training to make that, literally, a walk in the park. There was a backup Plan B, and even a Plan C for today's operation, but thankfully it never came to that.

But what a godsend the ice-cream cart was. And the fact the vendor was a scrawny little runt the kidnapper's grannie could have taken down. He'd used a classic manoeuvre practised a thousand times. A lightning-fast heel kick to the bloke's knee, catch his head on the way down, and then a sharp upward diagonal twist of the noggin, the last element delivering a satisfying crunching sound. The bloke dropped like a stone. He was either dead or in a coma. Disabled for life if he ever woke up, poor bugger. No time to check though. Collateral damage was always regrettable, but nothing would stand in the way of getting the job done.

He'd watched Lisbon high-tail it around the corner. The clock was ticking and everything had to go right. Lisbon was no dummy, but they were smarter. He had a niggling doubt the woman would pull off the act, despite the boss's reassurance. He was ready for the alternative plans, but not keen on them. Plan A was the best. But she was a champion, played an Oscar-winning performance that got the crowd running from all directions. As expected, Lisbon instructed his daughter to stay put, not knowing what kind of danger lay where the primal scream had come from. As a caring parent, he'd likely reason there could be a terrorist or a knife-wielding maniac hacking at passers-by. This park had seen its share of loonies over the years.

The lassie was unconscious inside the capacious ice-cream bin. He'd dumped the contents – several hundred pounds worth of cold treats – behind a hedge of azalea bushes, right next to the body of the real ice-cream vendor, health status unknown.

He chuckled as he watched a couple of teen boys struggling with a canoe stuck in some reeds. He called out good luck, they told him to piss off. He chuckled again.

The snatch itself was easier than he anticipated. A nice kid, she turned out to be. And nice kids are always the most trusting.

'Here love,' he'd said gently, a coin glinting in his extended hand. 'Your dad forgot to take his change when he bought the choc ices.' He approached with quick steps, knowing there wasn't much time. He fingered the hat as if to signal *See. I'm legit.*

She squinted one eye and frowned. 'I thought he said to keep the change? It was only a couple of pence.'

'Company policy.'

'And you weren't the man who served us.'

'Change of shift.' He edged behind her. 'Did you drop a hanky?'

Skye half-turned her head, but too late. He'd placed the cloth to her nose and pressed hard, adjusted his grip to apply the wrestling move to render her unconscious. The pressure had to be just right – less than he'd apply to an adult — or he risked killing her. *Not an option!* The boss's words rang in his ears.

The girl struggled hard for a moment, feisty and tough like her father was said to be. A hundred metres away, the woman continued with her act. Thankfully, it was a show-stopper that distracted everyone within earshot. Everyone but the kidnapper.

Chapter Eight

'YOU GOT THE PARCEL?'

'Yes, mate,' Ice-cream man muttered. 'I texted you that I had. You been asleep at the wheel?'

'No.' The driver's croaky voice was laden with exasperation. 'I got the text. I'm double checking. Anything could have happened en route. Correct?'

Ice-cream man shook his head. 'Unlikely. I'm a bloody professional. Five years in the army special forces. You need to trust me more.'

The driver let the response hang in the air, opened the rear door of the 2014 Ford Transit Connect. Inside squatted Frisbee thrower, now dressed in navy-blue overalls to match the driver. She nodded at the two men, expressionless as a department store mannequin.

The getaway van, adorned with the logo of a fake plumbing company complete with fake phone number, was parked under shady trees that hung out halfway across the road – privacy from intrusive security cameras guaranteed.

The two men were obliged to wait thirty seconds for a pizza-delivery cyclist to ride by. Once he'd disappeared around a corner, Ice-cream man extracted Skye from the freezer hold and handed the unconscious girl to the woman. The driver resumed his place behind the wheel, started the engine, gave two taps on the gas pedal. *Let's get a move on, please.*

The woman held the girl in outstretched arms as if she weighed no more than a loaf of bread, then carefully placed her on a thin mattress. She rested a hand on Skye's brow. The residual frigid air inside the food compartment had turned Skye's skin ice cold. The woman glared at Ice-cream man. 'Christ, she's frozen stiff! You sure she's going to be OK?'

He nodded quickly. 'Don't stress, Suzie. Not enough time elapsed to cause any harm. It's about -18°C in a domestic freezer, that smaller one would be in the same ballpark. I turned it off immediately, so the temperature would've been rising, especially with the body heat. And she's in a puffer jacket. Humans can survive extraordinary conditions, you know. She'll wake up later and have no knowledge of it.' Thermophysics lecture over, he clambered into the rear of the van, applied cable ties around Skye's ankles and wrists. He checked her pulse – steady and regular, took off the gag and listened for her breathing – normal. A quick inspection of her neck revealed he'd been precise with his technique – no bruising. He palpated the surrounding areas, found no physical damage. He snapped off a portrait photo of Skye on his burner phone, sent it to the boss on another burner phone. Those devices and those in the possession of the driver and Suzie would be at the bottom of the sea by the end of the day. He smiled wanly and returned to the van's passenger seat, leaving Suzie to play nurse and guard all at once.

MINDFUL not to disobey a single road rule, even the minor ones the cops don't generally care to enforce, the driver checked the mirror, looked over his shoulder, indicated, and sedately moved into the driving lane. Soon the van exited onto a major road and the driver pushed a button to lower the window. He lit a cigarette and blew a mouthful at the windscreen. The passenger followed suit. Enough noxious fumes filled the cabin to set off an industrial smoke alarm.

'Damn, I needed this ciggie,' said Ice-cream man. 'My nerves are shot to pieces.'

'Really, Mr Professional? Didn't you serve in all the hotspots in Afghanistan?'

'Yeah, but that was different. Everything I did was sanctioned by the army. I broke no laws.'

'You killed other men over there, didn't you?'

A deep drag followed by a nod. 'I machine-gunned three suspected terrorists in a raid outside of Jalalabad. Turned out they were shepherds sheltering in a stone hut. Made a horrible mess.'

'Jesus Christ.'

'I've never lost any sleep over it. The orders came from "on high", as they say. Not my fault the intelligence was shite. But if anything bad happens to this little one...I dunno...I reckon I'd lose my mind.'

'But snatching her's OK, is it?'

'Listen, I ain't getting into any moral arguments with you of all people. This will all turn out fine. Just shut up and drive.'

'Sorry, mate. I'm wound up like a spring myself.' The driver flicked the butt of his cigarette out the window. 'Let's just try and relax and have faith in the process.'

'Sure. Let's get this over with.'

On their way past Hammersmith on the M4 motorway, the driver set the dash-mounted phone to hands free and dialled the boss. After five rings came an impatient 'What's happening?'

'Didn't you get the picture I sent you?' said Ice-cream man.

'No, I haven't checked yet. I've been busy setting up the secure cryptocurrency account. A lot more complicated than I thought it would be, but I had to make sure it was 100% untraceable.'

'Right. Well, good news. The penguin has landed.'

'Huh?'

'I'll explain later. Suffice to say, we'll see you soon with a special delivery.'

The boss gave a whoop. 'Great work, fellas. What's your ETA?'

'We've got plenty of provisions and our own fuel, so we'll be driving with virtually no stops apart from toilet breaks. I've pinpointed a number of secluded areas on the way. We'll be arriving as per schedule tomorrow morning.'

'Excellent.' The sound of mouse clicks and keyboard strokes. 'I've just added your photo of the kid to the ransom message and fired it off to Lisbon's phone.'

'How do you think he'll respond?' The driver lit another smoke.

'He can't. He can only receive messages.'

'What?'

'The only response I'll accept is half a million quid's

worth landing in the crypto account. I'm not engaging in a back-and-forth with him or the cops or anyone.'

'But how…?'

The conversation was interrupted by loud thumping and yelling from the back of the van. '*HELP! HELP!*'

The boss chuckled. 'She's awake, then?'

'Sounds like it,' said Ice-cream man. 'A feisty one.'

'You fellas made sure the vehicle was sound-proofed, yeah?'

'Of course.'

'Then don't worry about it. Just keep your collective cool.'

'*My dad's going to kill you bastards! He's going to—*'

'What is she saying?' said the boss.

'She said her dad's going to kill us,' said the driver. 'You think that's likely?'

The boss burst out laughing. 'No chance. He's friendless in the UK. Him against all of us? Gimme a break.'

'I dunno about that,' said Ice-cream man. 'I've had a bit of a sniff around and it seems lotsa people have come around to him after his heroic exploits in Australia. It was all over the news how he's caught a bunch of murderers.'

'Nah, no way,' the boss rebutted. 'My spies tell me it's not just him solving all the crimes. He's got a crack team of detectives working with him Down Under. But his old mates in London have abandoned him. They're still dirty on Lisbon for his corrupt ways. He's on his own here, believe me. Besides, the chump will never find out who we are! Drive carefully and I'll see you with the goods.'

The conversation ended and the driver flicked the radio to a commercial pop channel. A Bon Jovi classic. Both men waited for the chorus before belting out the words, getting the lyrics wrong like most people do. ♪ *Shot to the heart…* ♪

More thumping kicks from the rear of the van.

'At least the kid's not yelling any more.' The driver increased the volume. 'Suzie must've put the gag back on. Poor kid.'

'Yeah, and poor Suzie,' said the Ice-cream man. Both men burst out laughing before resuming 1980's Karaoke on the M40 motorway.

Chapter Nine

JACK'S solar plexus convulsed as he let go of the phone. The device bounced off the concrete path with an ominous sound. He bent to pick it up. A new lightning-bolt crack in the screen didn't prevent him from seeing the familiar image. Skye. Serene, with her eyes closed. He stroked the image on the phone. At first he thought she was wrapped in a sleeping bag, then he discerned it was one of those hideous full-length puffer jackets. Her skin seemed to be drained of its natural colour, pallid almost. *Oh my God, is she dead?* No! Surely no one hated him so much they'd kill the only person he really loved in this world.

He noticed there was an attachment. *Don't ever open attachments from unknown addresses.* DC Claudia Taylor, his partner back in Australia, warned him again and again about digital security. He'd had his credit card hacked on a holiday to the Gold Coast last year and lost over a thousand dollars before he cancelled the card. Her words had no effect this time. Skye was more important than a damned credit card.

Jack's heart raced along at full tilt. He pressed his shaky forefinger on the link to open the message. Instead of popping open, something downloaded and he had to search around for a minute before locating the PDF. His eyes darted left and right. He read it twice, one hand rubbing his sweaty forehead, before the reality of the situation sunk in.

Hello Jack,
We have your daughter. She is alive and well. If you want to see her again, deposit 20 Bitcoins into the following account: bc1qar0srrr7xfkvy5l643lydnw9re59gtzzwf5jsl.
You have until 20:00 hours, Tuesday 13 March, to make the payment. One minute late, and the consequences are too dire to contemplate.
You will not be able to contact us at any stage. Do not reply to this number, it is already redundant and inoperable. However, we will be watching you. Do not contact the police. Do not alert the press. Do not post on social media. *We will be watching.*
Upon receipt of the payment, you will receive further instructions.
Do as instructed and no harm will come to your daughter. Fail to do so and you will never see her again. Alive or dead. *Do not do anything stupid. We will be watching.*

Jack struggled to breath. He went to loosen his tie, then he remembered he wasn't wearing one. He tried to walk to *their bench*. His feet wouldn't obey his brain, he staggered and stumbled. People strolling by stared at him like he was drunk or on drugs or simply a loon. He grabbed the metal armrest, slowly lowered himself into the seat. Sweat leaked from every pore, drenching his underarms. His whole world was crumbling. *Think, Lisbon, think.*

There was so little time. He checked his watch. 4:47pm. A little over 52 hours. Not quite the movie cliché of 48 hours, but close. Against his instincts he decided the best policy was to pay the ransom. If it was someone else's kid, the strategy would be *never accede to their demands*. But there was too much risk attached, too many unknowns. Besides, it wasn't someone else's kid. It was his flesh and blood.

First obstacle: where was he going to get Bitcoin from? And what was that amount even worth? A hundred thousand quid? A million?

First things first. Keep Skye safe. And that meant… What did it mean? *Shit!* Now he knew Skye had been kidnapped, he needed to call off his volunteer helpers. Last thing he needed was for the word to spread that a child had been abducted. If the news somehow reached Sarah, everything would go totally pear shaped. First call, Roger.

'Yes?' came the eager response. 'Have you found her?'

'Ah, yeah. I'm so sorry. She got shitty with me for some reason and took the Tube back home.'

'Oh, great news! You must be so relieved.'

Silence.

'Are you there, Mr Lisbon?'

'Yes, I'm…ah…thrilled.' Jack remembered his earlier rude tone and switched tack. 'And thank you so much for assisting me. You are model citizens and…ah…yeah. So, good-bye and all the best.'

'Hang on, Mr—'

Jack disconnect the call. Hopefully the couple had had an exciting day and would go home and get on with their lives. Next, he rang the other man. Jack thanked him profusely and wished the family well.

Now what, Lisbon? No chance he'd be calling DCI Pedersen now. If the kidnappers were into Bitcoin, they'd also be experts in all kinds of fancy tracking technology. Maybe they were tracing his phone already. He'd need to be extra careful with communications from now on. What he needed to know most of all was this – how the hell would he make the transaction to the kidnappers? He hadn't a clue. His gut told him a bit of Googling wasn't going to offer up answers, and if it did they would be beyond his understanding. And how was he going to hide the fact his daughter was missing? If that got out, the press would be all over it and Skye would be…he shuddered to think.

And one more nightmare to add to the equation.

What was he going to say to Skye's mother?

Chapter Ten

'SARAH, hi. I'm taking the kid on a trip to Cornwall for the next couple of days. Pretty cool, huh? We'll have a smashing time and be back on Wednesday morning.' Jack had chosen to use his own phone for the call, local SIM. If the kidnappers were somehow eavesdropping, his efforts to keep a lid on the abduction would surely meet with their approval.

'You say wot, Jack Lisbon? I did *not* give you permission for dat. She got school to go to tomorrow, dammit.' The Jamaican accent had faded over the years, but anger reinstated its full poetic beauty. 'Put her on da phone immediately.'

'Sorry, Sarah. She's fast asleep at the moment.' His hand holding the phone shook so much he swapped it to the other hand. That one shook just as much, so he swapped it back again. His stomach roiled, he thought he was going to be sick. Water, he needed water, his mouth was so parched. He'd guzzle a whole bottle after this nightmare of a conversation. He'd toyed with the idea of full-disclosure but decided against it. With her unpredictable temperament and penchant for sharing, Sarah could unwittingly let the cat of the bag, tell the wrong people. Or she'd ignore the warnings and call the police. Either way, Skye would be doomed.

'Now you listen to me!' she ploughed on. 'Either you come home as planned this evening or I will report you for child abduction. I don't care if you da big hero detective these days, you understand me?'

Jack winced, gathered his thoughts. 'C'mon, Sarah. It'll give you a well-deserved break. You can hang out with your girlfriends from the salon, hit the bars, have a few cocktails.'

He could hear her short, shallow breaths slow down. The gears must be ticking over in her brain. The idea was tempting. She was about to cave.

'OK, but I want her to call me the minute you get to… where are you taking her again?'

Jack had to think for a second. 'Cornwall. A couple of days by the sea. It's not summer, but still, with global warning 'n that, anytime's a nice time by the sea, innit?'

'You're lucky I'm a soft touch. You ring me tonight when you arrive, you got me?'

'Will do.'

'One more thing. Where you gonna be staying at and how you gettin' there?'

He'd been prepared for this. 'It's off-shoulder season, so we'll have no trouble finding a hotel or Airbnb. And don't worry about a change of clothes or anything like that. We've been shopping. Stocked up on everything we need for our little holiday. If we've forgotten anything, we can buy it there, can't we Skye? Oh, I forgot she was asleep.' *Nice touch, Lisbon.* 'We're half way there already. London to Penzance, first class all the way.'

'My Skye deserves nothing less, having to put up wit a moron like you for two whole days. You take care of may baby now, or there'll be hell to pay. Do you hear me, Jack Lisbon!'

———

THERE WAS no time to savour the pyrrhic victory of his subterfuge over Sarah. His gut told him Micky Knox was the person to approach about figuring out how to pay the ransom. This morning on the phone he mentioned he'd completed an IT course. And, as he recalled, the lad had always been ahead of most of his rivals. Knox had been in many fearsome fights back in the day, but the lad's evasive skills were second to none over his years as an amateur boxer. Meaning he'd hit more than he'd been hit and his brain had escaped relatively unscathed. Jack's instinct was to trust no one anymore, but going this alone was out of the question. If he had to pick one ally out of the poor selection available to him, it would be Micky Knox.

A rapid text message exchange established Knox was at home, engaging in that mysterious "drop-shipping" activity. Jack convinced the lad to take a break from his labours, and meet at the gym, he had some important news. There was no point engaging in cloak-and-dagger games now – the bastards had struck and they'd struck hard. Might as well hide in plain sight, as the saying goes.

March to taxi rank. Wave hand at black cab. Get in.

'Had a good day?' the affable cabbie enquired as Jack clicked his seat belt.

'No, I ain't. And I'd prefer to ride in complete silence if you don't mind. And don't spare the horses.'

'Right you are, guv.' The cabbie tugged the front of his

peaked cap and drove off with squealing tyres. That was one of the great things about London – well-mannered, no-nonsense taxi drivers. The customer is king.

A careening fifteen-minute ride through half-deserted narrow streets took Jack to the gym. The density of housing and businesses in London was a mini culture shock after five years enjoying the wide-open expanses of Yorkville. There was more rubbish on the streets here, more graffiti, more air pollution, more noise. Despite the negatives, the place still pulled on his heartstrings.

Jack punched in the code he'd memorised that the lad used to let them in this morning. The place was quiet. He'd expected a much bigger crowd tonight. Sundays were usually the busiest day of the week. Folks wanted their muscles to be popping, primed to show off underneath close-fitting business clothes at the office on Monday morning. A poster near the free-weights area told him why the place was almost deserted. Millwall FC, the football team supported by most of McNair's regulars since the 1960s and blessed with the most belligerent fans in the history of English soccer, was playing arch rival West Ham at home tonight in an FA Cup elimination match. Jack felt sorry for the police officers who had to attend that one – it took very little to spark violence among fans at these grudge matches. Bottles, bricks and fists were the weapons of choice. Occasionally a hooligan would have a sneaky thrust with a switchblade. That mindless tribal violence was a part of London he would never miss.

Mickey Knox was tucked away out of sight, sitting on a stool just behind the raised boxing ring. The greasy mullet of yesteryear was gone, replaced by a stylish haircut, and his acne had cleared up nicely. His dress sense had improved, too. Button-down white shirt and pressed grey slacks teamed with shiny black brogues. Knox seemed to be enthralled by a couple of welter-weights slugging it out in a sparring contest that had a deal more sting in it than your average training session. The combatants clearly had some issues to resolve. Jack dragged a metal chair which scraped along the concrete floor, plonked it down next to Knox, spun it around and sat astride it like he was riding a horse.

Oof, came from behind the ropes closest to Jack and Knox. A powerful rip to the stomach had struck home perfectly. A saliva-coated mouthguard flew across the top rope, bounced next to Jack's feet. He grabbed it with a small towel someone had left behind and tossed it back into the ring. *Let's go again, orright?* said the smaller of the boxers. He ripped off a glove, wiped the mouthguard on his trucks, thrust it back in his mouth and squared up to his opponent. Hygiene be damned. The thumps and thwacks of blows to flesh continued.

'Christ on a bike, you look like you've got terminal cancer with a week to live,' said Knox, the alacrity in his tone jarring with the grim words. 'What's happened? And… oh, shit. Where's the kid?'

Jack rocked forward, held his head in his palms. 'Gone, mate. I should have listened to your warning. I was too cocky.'

Knox's eyebrows knitted together. 'What do you mean, gone?'

'Some fucker's taken her, innit? What a stupid idiot I am.' Jack meekly explained the ruse the kidnappers had used to distract him while they snatched Skye. It was embarrassing to have been fooled so easily.

'Don't be too hard on yourself, mate. It was a coordinated effort.'

Jack's face emerged from behind his hands. 'And how

would you know?' He glared at Knox, bared his teeth like a dog about to attack. Perhaps he was wrong to trust the bloke. 'A bit of a coincidence, hey? You calling me in the park and the next minute – bang – she's gone.' He reached across, applied a cobra-fast wrist lock on Knox. 'How did you fucking know?'

'Oi! Let go, you big ox!' He gestured with his head at the TV. 'Fifteen minutes ago this story came on the telly. Some poor bloke's been murdered in the park you've just come from.'

'What?' Jack released his grip, eliciting a sigh of relief from Knox.

'Yeah. An ice-cream seller was found in some bushes, broken neck. All his ice-creams were tossed out of the cart, which they found abandoned at the southern exit. Cops are swarming all over the place. Look.'

Jack watched a toothy female reporter from a dedicated news channel mouthing and pointing frantically. The sound was off, but closed captions were on. Jack read the rolling text for a minute before turning his attention back to Knox. 'So the redhead must've been working with whoever killed that poor bloke, the kidnapper's chucked Skye into the cart, and then…'

'Yeah, looks that way. Have you reported the kidnapping?'

'No chance. Here, look at this, sunshine.'

Knox read the message, eyes bulging like a goldfish. He let out a low whistle. 'Fuck me. Twenty Bitcoin. That's a lot of money.'

'How much?'

'I'd have to check, but I'd say well over half a million pound sterling.'

'I ain't got that kind of change lying about. Dammit! I

thought maybe a hundred thousand. I could arrange that, maybe. Not easy, but I could do it.'

Knox pursed his lips. 'Big-time crooks demand cryptocurrency as ransom payments when they hack into multinational businesses or government enterprises. It's becoming so common, firms have sprung up that specialise in processing the payments, which almost legitimises the crime, in my view. With ransomware attacks, it's the method of choice these days. The processing companies charge like wounded bulls. If the payment itself is beyond your reach, then using a third party to do the transaction isn't going to be an option either.'

Jack stared at Knox open mouthed. Was this the same two-bit scrapper he used to know? The lad who was so eager to help him commit a crime because he was desperate for cash? It was like Knox was speaking Mandarin instead of English.

'How come you know all this?'

'Jack, it's all thanks to you. Like I was trying to tell you before, I invested the cash you gave me in an IT course, improved myself through self-education and set up an import-export company.'

'Is that the drop-shipping malarky you mentioned?'

'Yeah. The best part about it is the fact I don't hold any inventory. I buy stuff online and redirect the goods to other punters at a higher price.'

'Classic middle-man operation.'

'Yep. I've also been studying up on Bitcoin and other cryptocurrency. It's a bleedin' hard concept to get your head around, but any businessman worth their salt will have to come to grips with it sooner or later. Some are predicting the end of cash within a generation or two. So as a businessman, I'm obliged to know all about it.'

'All very interesting, but the clock's ticking, my son. If I can't get the readies in this weirdo money, my little girl could die. You understand?'

Knox took a deep breath and stood up. 'I've got an idea. Let's go for a walk.'

'Where to?'

'My place. I want to show you something.'

KNOX LIVED in an apartment above a sex shop. To get to it, you had to walk through the shop itself. Jack didn't know where to look as he followed Knox past shelves stacked high with sex toys, lubricants, lingerie and bizarre objects whose purpose he couldn't even begin to guess at. He kept his gaze lowered, not keen to meet the eye of the two elderly male customers studying the covers of pornographic DVDs, nor the hair-twirling busty blonde serving behind the counter. They took a spiral staircase to a sparsely furnished studio flat.

Living space was only a couple of square metres. One sofa, which probably folded out to double as a bed, a couple of plastic chairs and a desk. A kettle and some cups on a bench and a small two-door wall cupboard. Jack had been in roomier caravans. The abundance of computers, spare parts, tools and cables, specialist IT magazines, sticky notes and various charts on the wall gave Jack confidence in Knox's abilities. The bloke was obsessed with his job and obsessed people were often experts in their field.

'I'm sorry about the cramped conditions.'

Jack waved the apology away. 'Son, people are living on the streets in their thousands. This flat would be a palace to them.'

'I'll never be one of them, guv. Here, check this out. I've just purchased this little beauty. I move in early April.' From nowhere Knox pulled out a glossy A4 printed page of a two-storey brick home with an address in St Albans, not far from Greater London. Price tag, £1.3 million.

'What the...?'

'I told you, guv. It's all down to you. I did an IT course, then another, set up my business, and I've been either studying or working ever since. Saved every penny. That's why I'm living all frugal like, you see?'

Jack scratched his head. 'You sure you haven't been indulging in, how can I put it, illegal activities?'

'Not at all, guv,' Knox shook his head. 'I have taken some risks with investing in stocks and securities, I'll admit, but never without proper evaluation of the companies whose shares I'm buying. I've built up my drop-shipping business to the point where it rakes in the money virtually on autopilot, which gives me more time to study the markets. And, more importantly, new technologies like Bitcoin and the like. Oh, and a bit of sports gambling. Especially the boxing.'

A deep breath from Jack. 'That's all well and good, Micky. Very laudable, in fact, and I'm proud of you beyond words. However, my main concern is getting Skye back.'

'That's what I wanted to show you.'

Knox booted up his PC before the screen-saver image appeared. A classic black-and-white image of Muhammad Ali in the middle of a boxing ring. He logged in and the desktop appeared, littered with perhaps a hundred folder icons. The cursor hovered over one near the middle. Inside was a video.

'Look, guv. I have always done everything above board in business. But I just had to save this little video I found online. I'm not sure what it teaches is strictly kosher. Wanna watch?'

The MP3 was a five-minute long clip entitled *Fake Bitcoin Wallets and Transactions*.

'Is it going to help get Skye back?' said Jack.

Knox started the video, Jack pulled up the second chair. 'Possibly.' Knox fetched two mugs from the cupboard. 'Tea or coffee?'

At the end of the video, Jack was one tea to the good, but no wiser as to the next step. 'What does it all mean? I thought blockchain was something they use to clear trees in the Amazon jungle.'

'Essentially, all you need to know is I know how to do it. And I'm prepared to do it for nothing. I'll send them twenty fake Bitcoins in exchange for Skye.'

'What if it goes wrong? What if they realise the coins are dodgy? What if the deadline passes and your efforts come to nothing? And…what if they don't keep their word?'

'Guv, there are no guarantees in this life. That's why I suggest you put together an alternative plan. One I'm also prepared to help you with.'

'And what's that?'

'Do what you do best. Detective work. Find the bastards who kidnapped your daughter and bring them to justice.'

Jack slammed his fist down on the desk, causing Knox's 28-inch screen to wobble crazily. 'Damn it you're right, son. Let's rattle some effing cages!'

'Where are you going to stay for the next two days?'

'Pardon?'

'On the walk over here you told me Sarah thinks you and Skye are in Cornwall. How are you going to sniff around the manor for clues without drawing attention to yourself?'

'Good point. I'll have to hide out somewhere.'

Knox pulled out the desk drawer, handed Jack two keys. 'What' this?'

'The house in St Albans. It's got some basic furniture. Beds, some chairs, not much else. You could crash there for a couple of days. Actually, I think there's some linen in a cupboard somewhere, not sure. Make it your HQ for the next two days.'

'Brilliant, thanks.'

'Give me your phone. I wanna check something.'

Jack handed it over without question. Knox plugged a cord into it, then the other end of the cord into a hub with a bunch of USB slots. An app appeared on the computer screen. Knox pressed a square button. In less than a minute he declared the phone bug free. 'This doesn't mean it will stay that way. But it's fairly easy to tell if your phone's been hacked into. You might notice clicking sounds, static or distant voices coming through your phone during conversations, the battery will deplete a lot faster. If you're in doubt use a payphone or borrow someone else's mobile. Most importantly, don't use the Internet on your phone.'

Jack nodded. Knox handed him an iPad. 'Here, use this if you have to look up anything online. Wi-Fi is already switched on at the St Albans house, so you're good to go.' He gave Jack the login and password.

'This is unbelievable. If you weren't making a killing I'm sure the London Met would pay handsomely to have you on their IT team.'

'I doubt it. There are others way smarter than me.' Knox offered a lopsided grin. 'One more thing.' Knox explained that Paddy Sheehan, the only other person in the world who knew for sure what Jack did to Alex Gallagher all those years ago, would assist in anyway possible. 'Don't get a swelled head, guv, but Paddy is in total awe of you, the way you turned your life around. I've also got a feeling your old buddy Lex Buskin would agree to lend a hand. He's always banging on about the cases you solved in Australia.'

Jack felt himself blushing. 'I'm hardly a bleedin' role model for anyone, sunshine.'

'Not even for Skye?'

'Maybe with that exception.'

Knox tapped a pen against his top teeth. 'I know the message said no cops, but is there someone in the force you could reach out to?'

'Only one. He's solid. I'm just terrified word will get back to the kidnappers if I don't do exactly as they say.' Jack was suddenly finding it hard to breathe. It was all well and good theorising with Knox about this and that, but the reality was Skye's life was in danger.

Knox ventured to put a comforting arm around Jack's shoulder. Lisbon didn't flinch. In fact, to his surprise, it calmed him. 'It's your call with the cop. As far as me and Paddy go, you have nothing to worry about.'

Jack cleared his throat. 'One thing bothers me.'

'Yeah, what's that?'

'How did the kidnappers get my number? I understand how you did, by stealing Gallagher's little black book. But my personal London number wasn't known to too many folk. In fact, only by a small circle of friends. I'm talking Polo Mint small.' Jack took a deep breath as a distant memory flickered then came into full view. 'You remember young Pete Bitetti?'

'Yes.'

'I'm pretty sure we exchanged phone numbers a few

weeks prior to the Gallagher incident. Pete had some real heavy drug issues and I was looking at getting him a counsellor. I never got back to him. He might resent me for that, want some payback.'

'Nah, I doubt it.'

'How can you be sure?'

'He died of a heroin overdose two years ago. His family abandoned him, he had no friends. Sad.'

'OK. Scratch him. But something else just occurred to me. You've just shown me the phone's clear of bugs. Excellent. But the cops can still track the movement of the phone even with data switched off, correct? Cell phone triangulation.'

'True. Are you thinking someone in the police might be involved in this?'

Jack pursed his lips and shook his head. 'Fuck knows. I had a lot of enemies in the Met. And for good reason. I was a corrupt son of a bitch. I can imagine some of them'd be fuming I've made good in Australia while they're stuck in a rut.'

Knox reached into the drawer again, rifled around for a moment. 'Here.' He held out an old style silver Nokia N95 complete with charging kit. 'Use this. You can toss it in the Thames later. Keep your own phone handy for backup. Keep it switched off, but check it now and again to see if the kidnappers have left any messages.' Knox offered a smile of encouragement.

'Gotcha.'

'Before you switch that phone off, forward me the message with the link in it. I'm gonna need the account number the kidnappers provided for the transaction.'

For the next fifteen minutes Jack manually re-entered contacts of people he may need to call over the next two days. Then he plugged in the charger until the device was primed and ready to go.

'So, what's your next move?' said Knox.

'My gut tells me whoever did this is either a cop I used to work with, or someone close to Gallagher out for revenge with a bonus payoff. Also, when you called me earlier to warn me bad things could happen, you suggested Gallagher's kids didn't hate their old man like everyone thinks. That came as news to me. I'd like to get some eyeballs on Cedric and Alicia. At least it's a place to start.'

'But how? You can't just rock up and question people like you would in a normal enquiry where you're not the victim.'

'Don't I know it! The only way forward I can see is for me to co-ordinate the operation from your digs in St Albans with you and Sheehan, possibly Buskin, and my friend in the Met assisting on the ground. Kind of like a male version of Charlies Angels.'

'Whose angels?'

'Never mind. You're too young.'

'Oh, right.'

Knox collected the mugs, rinsed them under the tap. Tea towel in hand he said, 'You reckon your copper pal will help out?'

Jack tossed two pellets of Extra gum in his mouth. 'I bleedin' hope so.'

Chapter Eleven

THE STRONG TAKE-AWAY double espresso was exactly what he needed. The brew, picked up en route from a service station not far from Knox's St Albans digs, got the synapses in Jack's brain firing. That and the added pressure of the clock. Fifty-two hours had quickly turned into forty-four. It was now midnight and Jack's mind was racing. He sat bent over sheets of paper spread across the kitchen table, writing down ideas as they came to him. Half of them were nonsensical, some had merit. The result was chicken scratch Scotland Yard's best handwriting expert would have trouble deciphering.

The situation was desperate, but not as desperate as it had been six hours prior.

Now, he had some allies. Two would be based in London – Knox and Sheehan, and the third, Lex "Bruiser" Buskin, swore to stay by his side for the duration, do whatever he could to help crack the case.

Bruiser, sitting to Jack's right in the kitchen of the sprawling, near-empty house, read from the Dell laptop he'd brought with him. He was scanning the list of people involved in the Gallagher murder enquiry – suspects and investigators. He'd found a handful of public domain reports and news articles and entered in a spreadsheet the names of those he thought worth a further look. Jack felt he could trust the man's judgement on this; Bruiser was a stock market trader with a mathematics degree and a healthy portfolio, clearly no fool.

Without a second's hesitation Bruiser had agreed to assist as man-on-the-ground while Jack remained inside the safehouse, only venturing outside for exercise. Who knew what spies were about? He picked up Jack in his red Jaguar XFS in a quiet side street two blocks from the gym, and from there it was a thirty-minute drive to Knox's house. The men were about the same build, so Bruiser grabbed a couple of changes of clothes for Jack, and some basic toiletries. The man was recently divorced and living on his own, so he could do what he wanted when he wanted, no explanations. His job would be to run errands, interview people, spy, stake out, whatever Jack needed.

Two years before Jack departed the UK with his tail between his legs, he'd played a handful of squash games with Bruiser. The man's regular doubles partner had a massive heart attack. Jack played three matches as fill-in while the patient recuperated, but the makeshift pair lost heavily each time. Bruiser's partner took several months to fully recover but it quickly became apparent Jack was a poor choice and Bruiser found another substitute. It turned out that as a squash player, Jack was a great boxer. The upshot of all this, Bruiser was conveniently still among Jack's phone contacts from the old days.

'No bleedin' wonder your mate had a coronary, Lex. I read somewhere that squash is the sport most likely to give you a heart attack while playing it. A dozen people a year die on the court.'

'What?'

'Yeah, it was in a report from the NHS.'

A shadow passed over Lex's face. 'I was thinking of giving it away, as it happens. But look here. I've gone through all the files and broken down people into three categories, low, medium and high likelihood of being involved in the kidnapping of your daughter. Of course, at the end of the day, none of them might be implicated.'

'Good work, mate. What have you found for me?' Jack plucked a piece of pepperoni pizza from a box they'd had delivered to the house. He'd neglected to eat all day apart from the ice-cream in the park, mainly because his state of worry meant he couldn't stomach food. Eventually, the demands of his body gave in. 'Give me the high likelihood ones.'

Bruiser put down a half-eaten slice of pizza. He had none of Jack's appetite issues; he'd already tucked away three slices, some garlic bread and half a large bottle of Pepsi. 'I've whittled it down to eight names. They are: your immediate superior Superintendent Dave Keogh, former partners DI Jim Blackadder and DCI Brian Keddie, Cedric and Alicia Gallagher, and boxers from the gym, Alan Arment, Tony Sabra and Elrod Smart, who were involved in the scrap with you. Knox was a participant in the fight, too, but not on the list for obvious reasons.'

'I've seriously pissed off many more than that over the years. But what you've got there aligns with what I was thinking. Although you missed an important one.'

'Who?'

'The lead investigator, DI Chris Dreyfus. He had me squarely in the frame.'

'Nope. I looked into him. It seems after you left the country he changed his mind about you being a suspect.'

'He did?' Jack whistled through his teeth. 'How did I miss that?'

Bruiser turned the laptop around for Jack to see. Th DI's change of mind was fairly recent, July last year. He spoke about it in a newspaper interview Jack had missed. Not surprising, since he wasn't following news stories about Gallagher's murder as closely as he used to.

'Well done, sunshine. Got anything else?'

Before Bruiser could respond, Jack's burner phone rang. Number withheld. What the hell? Surely the kidnappers weren't onto them already? He handed the phone to Bruiser. 'Here, answer this, will ya. My heart's pounding fit to explode.'

Bruiser pressed the phone to his ear. 'Yes? OK, one second.' He passed the Nokia back. 'It's that Lars friend of yours from the Met.'

Jack snatched the phone. 'Lars? Oh my God, am I glad you called back. Is your phone secure?' He worked out how to put the outdated device on loudspeaker so Bruiser could hear the conversation.

'Of course it's secure. What's up, Jack? Your message sounded urgent.'

'Couldn't be more urgent, sunshine. My daughter's been kidnapped.'

'Holy shit! When?'

'About seven hours ago.'

'Did you report it officially?'

'They've threatened to kill her if I even contact the police, so you have to promise me you won't escalate the matter. Do you promise?'

'Absolutely. What can I do, mate?'

'The main problem is, we don't know the identity of the kidnappers. They've sent me a message with a ransom demand and—'

'Send it to me. I've got an IT genius in my department. Absolutely knows the meaning of discretion. He might be able to crack the location of where the message was sent from.'

'Want me to do that now? I have to get it from another phone.'

'It can wait for the moment. Fill me in on the facts first.'

Jack described in as much detail as he could the events in the park, the plan to carry out a fake cryptocurrency transaction, and revealed he had three other people assisting him.

'The murder of the ice-cream vendor in the park has to be linked,' said Lars. 'It's one of our top priorities on the manor.'

'It *is* linked, no doubt in my mind. The poor bloke was collateral damage in the kidnapping. Any leads on the murder from your officers?'

'One. Not a strong one, though. An old lady feeding ducks came forward after seeing the news on the TV this evening, said she'd seen a well-built white male pushing the cart by the river.'

'Was it the same one you found abandoned? I saw two other carts in the park.'

'It was.' Lars cleared his throat. 'Lemme just check the case notes on the server. Yes, the description of the man the pensioner saw was vastly different from the two other ice-cream vendors. One was an Asian male, the other a white female, both shorter than the potential suspect.'

'Any forensics at the scene?'

'Some boot prints and a tiny amount of fabric. No

finger prints, the kidnapper must've been wearing gloves. The victim had a snapped neck, which isn't easy to do unless you've had specialist combat training. Very professional. And...wait a minute...curly black hairs were found in the ice-cream cart's storage bin.'

'Oh my God!' Jack's pulse rate accelerated as he fought back tears. 'That's gotta be Skye's hair. The bastards put her in a bloody freezer, dammit!'

'Kidnappers are the absolute scum of the Earth, Jack. They'll do what's necessary to get their money, just bear that in mind. Don't expect–'

'If you're trying to reassure me, it ain't working.'

'I'm just being realistic.'

'Yeah, I understand. Get back to the...oh, Jesus...the hair you found.'

'At first glance it appears it could be Skye's. But we can't determine age or sex from hair unless the root's attached. I guess the DNA results will take a couple of days.'

'I don't need DNA tests to tell me what I already know. I'm going to make those arseholes pay for this! Was there blood in the cart? Please, Lars, tell me there was no blood!'

'No, there was no blood found. Try to calm down, Jack. I know it's not easy.'

Jack wiped a stray tear from under his eye, took a couple of deep breaths. 'OK, all good now. Did any witnesses describe the woman I told you about? The one who claimed to have been attacked by her boyfriend? She was a diversion to get me away from Skye.'

'No one mentioned such a woman. I'll put her description in a press release, shall I? Say she's a person of interest?'

'No! That would make the kidnappers think I've made a report.' Jack took a deep breath. 'I know you ignoring this information is technically undermining the investigation into the man's murder, but let me tell you, we find the kidnappers, we find the man's killer. Got me?'

'Yes, Jack. But you have put me in a rather compromising position. I'm not sure...'

'Listen, Lars! Please. If Skye dies because of me giving away too much information, it won't bring the other bloke back to life, will it?'

Silence for a moment.

'OK, Jack. What do you want me to do?'

'Check up on the lads who were in the dust-up with me the day Gallagher died. Except for Knox, he's working with me on this. More importantly, I want you to hack into the phones and computers of my old boss Dave Keogh and detectives Blackadder and Keddie. They've all got motive to see me suffer. See if you can find any compromising stuff on them.'

A sarcastic laugh. 'Jack, you can't be serious. I'm not sure I can authorise something like that. For one thing, Keogh's retired.'

Bruiser scribbled something on a piece of paper, spun it around to show Jack and tapped on what he'd written. 'Listen, Lars. I've found out some things about the three of them.'

'What?'

'Financial stuff. Keogh's amassed a fortune not commensurate with his salary, and the other two have had some serious accusations of corruption levelled at them. Taking bribes to cover big debts.'

Jack heard the sound of a drink going down Pedersen's gullet. 'So what? Blackadder and Keddie are suspended pending a thorough investigation. Personally, I think they're victims of an internal vendetta in the Met. As for Keogh, well, he got a bloody gong from the Palace last year for his services to Queen and country. He made his money through speaking engagements. The bloke's in high demand, let me tell you.' Pedersen sighed, or perhaps it was a yawn. 'I can't go spying on these people. Even if I *had* grounds, there's a process. It all takes time. Longer than the deadline the kidnappers gave you. What you're asking for is fantasy land stuff, Jack.'

'They all had it in for me, Lars. Keogh included. I don't care if he got a bleedin' knighthood or whatever. All of them could be behind this act. Blackadder in particular, he hounded me through the Gallagher investigation, accused me of all sorts of rubbish. Can you just set your sights on him, at least?'

'No, Jack. I can't. Here's what I am prepared to do. You mentioned someone asking questions about you around the gym, right?'

'Said his name was McTaggart. Could be an alias, of course.'

'I'll send a constable around there to grab security footage from that day. Who's the manager?'

'Woman called Cynthia, apparently.' Jack observed Bruiser nodding enthusiastically. 'Yep, that's who it is. I've not had the pleasure of meeting her. In fact, I'm not even sure who owns the place these days.' Bruiser shrugged. He didn't know either.

'Doesn't matter,' said Pedersen. 'We'll run the video through our face recognition software. If he's a baddie with a record, we'll have a chance of nailing him that way.' Another sip of something. 'You know, he could've simply been a geezer interested in meeting the great Detective Jack Lisbon.'

'Very flattering, Lars. But it's way too coincidental. Find

him and the actors from the park, and we find our effing kidnappers.'

'Possibly.' The sound of a lighter sparking, Pedersen drawing on a cigarette. Jack yearned for one, his old habit tapping in his brain, asking to come in. 'How has your ex taken the news? She'll be in total shock I imagine.'

'I ain't told her yet.'

'You what?'

'She thinks I'm with Skye in Cornwall for two days.'

'You're a brave man, Lisbon. I met your Sarah. She'll tear you to strips when she finds out.'

'I know. I called her earlier to tell her we'd arrived in Penzance and she wanted to talk to Skye. I had to use some fancy footwork to get out of that one. I said we'd had a row and she was sulking in the hotel bathroom and wouldn't come out.'

'You've always been the creative type, Jack.'

'Thanks, I think.'

'Now listen. There are specialists in this area. Are you sure you don't want me to get our best minds on this case? We can investigate in a clandestine and covert manner, taking care not to alert the kidnappers, whoever they may be.'

'That's the point though, innit? We don't know who the hell we're dealing with! I'm Skye's best chance of surviving this nightmare. I just need a little bit of assistance to unearth them, and you're the only copper I trust.'

'Fair enough, Jack. But going cowboy like this could backfire.'

'It won't.' Please, God, don't let it backfire.

Jack bade good-night to Pedersen, disconnected the call. He switched on his Samsung, forwarded the ransom message to the DCI as he'd requested, turned the phone off again as per Knox's recommendation. He turned to Bruiser, eyes drooping. 'What did you make of that? I hoped he would've been a bit more co-operative.'

'To be honest, even though he's your mate, his hands are tied.' Bruiser spoke in a conciliatory tone. 'Don't take this the wrong way, but I reckon you should be grateful for any help he can give you.'

Jack sighed, slammed down the remains of his stone-cold coffee. His watch told him it was past 1:00am. Another hour down, perhaps a step closer with Pedersen on board. The idea of face recognition software gave him hope. McTaggart was a big man. It was a big man pushing the ice-cream cart. Perhaps...

'Jack,' he felt a tap on the shoulder. 'You awake?'

'What?' Seconds earlier he'd been on high alert. The drama of the day had drained his energy reserves, his body craved sleep. 'Tell me... ah, geez...I can barely think, sunshine.'

A hand was gripping Jack's shoulder, the other around his waist, hoisting him out of the chair. 'Get some rest,' said Bruiser. 'You're exhausted.' He guided Jack up a set of thickly carpeted stairs and into an expansive room. On the floor was a queen-size mattress topped with a fluffy duvet. Barely conscious of his surroundings, Jack sat on the side of the bed, pulled his shirt off and tossed it into a corner, lay down and pulled the duvet up to his chin. A light clicked off, sending the room into darkness, and he fell into a deep, dreamless sleep.

Chapter Twelve

HE AWOKE WITH A JOLT, soaked in sweat. He looked at his watch, the glowing hands of his old-school timepiece telling him it was 4:03am. For a moment, he had absolutely no idea of his whereabouts. A slow and hazy realisation. Knox's house. St Albans. Yes, that's right. Then, the awful truth struck home.

Skye was missing and he had to find her.

The sound of loud snoring from across the hallway reminded Jack he had company. Bruiser was a good ally to have, but there was one person in the world he wished was by his side more than any other.

Jack took a minute-long shower in the massive en suite. Only a hand-towel, but he didn't care. He'd learned from beach swimming in Australia you can put your clothes straight back onto a wet body and it's no big deal. In fact, it was his partner who gave him the tip.

A quick mental calculation told him it was 2:03pm in Yorkville. The perfect time to give her a call. The phone rang and rang and rang. He was about to hang up when she answered.

'Detective Constable Claudia Taylor speaking.'

'Hey, Claudia.' *Cough, cough.* 'It's me, Jack.'

'You're sounding croaky. Has the born-again teetotaller had a relapse?' He heard a car's indicator clicking. 'It must be the middle of the night there. Miss me that much, did you?'

Her cheery, sultry voice would normally set his alpha male heart aflutter. Not this time.

'Nah. I just needed to talk to someone familiar. Everyone here seems like a stranger.'

'Even Skye?' Her voice was incredulous.

Jack rubbed his eyes, finding it hard to frame the words. 'No. Not her.'

'Good to hear. That was the whole point of you travelling back to—'

'She's been kidnapped, Claudia! I'm shit scared something's going to happen to her. I'll never be able to live with myself if they hurt my little girl.'

'Whoa, whoa back it up a bit. Did you say…wait a minute. Did you say she's been kidnapped?'

'It's all my fault. I got sucked in like a chump, they pounced and now I have no idea where she is.'

'What are the police doing?'

'Officially, nothing. I'm sorting it.'

'Holy shit, Lisbon. Are you serious? What would you advise a member of the public to do if their child was taken, huh?'

'I'd, ah…'

'You damn well know what you'd do. You'd tell them to call the cops and get the entire force behind the investigation. No ifs, buts or maybes.'

'Maybe.'

'I said no maybes!'

If not for the gravity of the situation, Jack would have said *touché*. He slowly rose from the bed and began pacing the room. Coffee, he needed coffee.

'You still there?' said Claudia.

'Yeah. I'm heading downstairs to get a brew. Hey, did the UK number display your end?'

'Yes.'

'Call me back on it in five, can you?'

'Sure.

Black instant coffee steaming, Jack fired up the iPad Knox had provided. Scanned the Internet for news, then turned on his own mobile to check for updates from the kidnappers. Nothing. The ice-cream man's murder and more of the endless wave of class actions against Big Pharma companies dominated. The mug of uninspiring coffee was halfway to Jack's lips when the phone burst into life. The +61 prefix alone made him homesick for Australia. 'Thanks for calling back.'

'You better have a good plan if you're going all Liam Neeson on this one.'

'I admit I don't have the black ops training he had. Or his character at least. But I'm going to get her back! I've enlisted help.' Jack described the ragtag team he'd assembled.

'For someone with trust issues, you've hitched your wagon to some dodgy characters there.'

'Desperate times, desperate measures and all that.'

'What about this DCI Pedersen? You sure he's reliable?'

'Almost 100%. He heads the Specialist Crime Command and has one of the best clean-up rates in the UK. He's the only officer who stayed friends with me after I left the Met four years ago, despite all the scuttlebutt. We email each other from time to time. He's a good man.'

'Jack, why don't you contact the National Crime Agency? They've got a unit called the Anti Kidnap and Extortion Unit.'

'How do you know that?' The name was new to Jack.

'I looked it up before I called you back.'

Jack shook his head and smiled to himself. He should have known she'd be researching the matter. 'Just a sec while I check 'em out.' He performed a quick internet search and found the agency's website. Established just after Jack left Great Britain, the NCA was a well-resourced and powerful instrument with global reach, as well as partnerships with international agencies like the FBI. Should he just hand over the case to them? 'I'm surprised Pedersen never mentioned this mob.'

'Probably because you told him you didn't want full-blown assistance. Correct?'

'Yes. And besides, I don't want to be dealing with some government organisation I've only just heard of. Know what I mean?'

'No, I don't know what you mean. Surely getting your daughter back is the most important thing? Is this more about your pride and exacting revenge?'

'For fuck's sake, Claudia! Of course it's about saving Skye. That's not what I meant. These shadowy agencies, I don't trust 'em. Operatives who charge into dangerous settings with guns blazing, risking a hostage's life because nabbing the perps is more important. I've been in a hostage situation myself, remember?'

'Yes, and you were the bloody hero. Who could ever forget?' The sarcasm wasn't lost, even from across the oceans.

'Correct. And not because I was cocky, but because I calmly assessed the situation and acted accordingly. No hostages were hurt. I can't guarantee that won't happen here. And you know why?'

'Tell me.'

'Because I saw the glint in the eyes of some of the grunts in the Special Emergency Response Team that eventually stormed the bank I was in. I saw how twitchy they were, too eager to pull the trigger. Skye could get caught in cross-fire. These things have been known to happen. Heard of that school in Beslan, Russia? Nearly two-hundred children killed. A complete disaster despite the involvement of so-called specialists. I could list many more examples. Wanna hear 'em?'

'All right, Jack. I get your point. I disagree with you, but...'

'But what?'

'Of all the people I've ever met, if anyone can pull this off, it isn't Liam Neeson. It's you.'

'Don't be daft.' The praise made his skin tingle. 'Can I ask you a favour?'

'Go ahead.'

'I've got some smart cookies helping me here, but can you do a bit more research for me from that end?'

'Of course. What do you want me to do?'

Jack gave her the names of the people on Bruiser's list and asked her to dig deep. He reasoned no one would be looking over Claudia's shoulder if she explored the records of these people, plus she'd have the resources of the globally connected Queensland Police Service to draw on.

'Will do,' said Claudia. 'Anything else?'

'Pedersen asked me who the manager of McNair's gym was these days and I was hard pressed to recall. Made me think perhaps other details about McNair's could be important. Like, who owns it, stuff like that. There's been rumours going around that relatives of the notorious Kray twins are part owners.'

'Why do you think that's important?'

'Somehow I think it's the key to everything. That Scottish bloke McTaggart came looking for me there. And it's where I...ah...had that dust up with Gallagher.'

'And where he was killed. You under the microscope over that for a while as a possible suspect as I recall.'

'Yeah, but I was rightfully cleared. The bastards turned me inside out trying to frame me but came up empty.' He tut-tutted himself for the overly defensive tone in his reply. He heard the echo of multiple car horns blaring in the background.

'What did you say, Jack, I missed it? There's a spot of road rage going on here. It's been stinking hot and the people are touchy.'

'I said thanks for being a pal.' God, that sounded corny.

'No worries. I'll get back to you in a few hours, let you know what I found.'

As he disconnected the call, the sound of soft footsteps behind him sent a shot of adrenaline through his body. Jack instinctively jumped out of his seat, spun around and adopted a boxer's stance, ready for combat. Bruiser stood there, bathrobe half open revealing more than Jack wanted to see. Still, the fact it wasn't an intruder drew a sigh of relief.

'Jesus, mate. You had me worried.'

'You should be. Come and see what I found.'

Chapter Thirteen

'WHAT THE HELL'S going on with all these cameras?' Jack turned on the loudspeaker and sat Bruiser's silver iPhone 12 in the middle of the floor. He and Bruiser had retreated to an empty utilities room, one of the few apparently not under surveillance.

'What? Is that you, Jack?' said Knox.

'Yeah.'

'What did you say again? It's... a quarter past six in the morning!'

'The cameras, sunshine. They're everywhere. We didn't notice at first, but Lex happened to look up at the corner of the ceiling in his bedroom. He spotted a tiny light blinking in the darkness, no bigger than a pinprick. We've just gone from room to room and found them all over the house. If you are part of this kidnapping, son, I would NOT want to be in your shoes, you hear me?'

'Oi, calm down. Are you delirious?'

'Far from it.' Jack shot a glance at Bruiser, who gave him

a nod of encouragement. 'We're simply on high alert. Especially now. What gives?'

'Nothing gives. I'd forgotten about them, that's all. When I bought the place the agent told me there'd been a spike in burglaries in the neighbourhood, so I got those cameras put in. I've also got external ones. They may be on, but they're not plugged into anything yet. So nothing's being recorded.'

'Oh,' said Bruiser, letting out a breath. 'I guess that's all right then. Gave me a scare, though.'

No wonder, thought Jack. Wandering around the place with your family jewels on display. Then, an idea. 'Are you able to get them to record remotely?'

'Sure. Just a couple of mouse clicks. You've changed your tune quickly.'

Jack scratched an armpit, looked over at the kettle. Another instant coffee would be needed to get the brain firing on all cylinders. After that he'd send Bruiser on an errand for a decent espresso. 'As long as we're aware of what gear's installed in the house, I'm fine with that. But it may as well be operational, just in case we get any unwelcome visitors.'

'Just a second.' The sound of a chair scraping, some buzzing and whirring sounds. 'There. All done. Bruiser, your hair looks frightful. You might need to put some gel in it or something before you face the world today.'

'So you can see us now?' Bruiser's hand shot up to his messed up blonde locks.

'Clear as day. The cameras are also armed with infrared sensors, so if any intruders break in at night, they'll be captured on the recording. You both familiarised yourselves with the alarm system, yeah?

Both men replied in the affirmative. A complex 10-digit

alphanumeric code, but thanks to their respective vocations, the pair had good heads for memorising such things. The code was also entered in their phones backwards in case of sudden amnesia.

'If that's all then, I'm going back to bed for a couple of hours. I was up late organising the Bitcoin transaction and I'm beat.'

Jack thanked him profusely.

'Part of the process was tricker than I'd anticipated,' Knox continued. 'But we're all ready to make the fake payment at the appointed hour. In fact, with your blessing, I'd like to push the button fifteen minutes before the deadline. Just in case.'

'In case what?' said Jack, doubts about Knox's abilities creeping into his mind. 'There can be no "in case". It has to work!'

'I'm confident it will. I was thinking along the lines of a power surge or something like that. The likelihood of that is minuscule. Rest assured, I've covered all contingencies.'

Again, Jack could barely credit this was the same Micky Knox talking. Five years ago he was a second-rate wanna-be fighter who could barely string a sentence together. It was amazing what ambition and an education can do to a person. Not getting punched in the head on a regular basis also helps.

'Sorry for my outburst, sunshine. Excellent work and all that. Are you up for another job?'

'Depends what it is.'

'Digital sleuthing. Looking into people's bank accounts, driver's licences and the like. Whatever you can find, basically.'

Bruiser carried two mugs of coffee back from the kitchen, drawing an appreciative half-smile from Jack.

'Ah, perhaps I gave the wrong impression,' said Knox with an apologetic tone in his voice. 'I'm not a programmer or a computer hacker. I've got some IT skills, but that's about it. I'm sorry.'

Jack sighed. It was too much to hope for. 'OK, Micky. How about some good old-fashioned legwork.'

'I'm up for that. The weather's lovely and I've got no appointments. What do you want me to do?'

Chapter Fourteen

Monday, 7:00am, McNair's Gym

ELROD SMART SQUARED up to the heavy bag, bounced up and down, slapped his gloves together. Warmup over, his muscles felt loose and strong. The gym was abuzz with activities: the clank of weights, the tappity-tappity-tap of the speed ball, groans, heavy breathing, and old-fashioned cursing. Smart blocked it all out, focused his attention on the cracked leather bag. Dukes raised up by his face, elbows high, palms facing outwards, he imagined he was a champion Muay Thai fighter. He'd never tried the style in a contest, but he was a big fan. His chosen form of unarmed combat was boxing.

For eight years Smart had been coming to McNair's to train before work. He'd had so many employment gigs over the years he couldn't remember them all, but he was never out of a job for long. Working class to the core and not ashamed. Taking unemployment benefits, that was shameful. In an hour he'd be rocking up to his shift at McDonald's. Not the most glamourous job, but it paid the bills and kept him out of trouble.

Making it big in boxing had been the dream, but the goal eluded him. He'd fought many fights, winning a lot of them, but never the ones that counted the most. These days he trained for fitness. And lately, it was just solo sessions. He'd lost the ability to socialise. If someone wanted to spar with him, he'd always decline politely. If not for the outlet of intense physical exercise, he probably would have fallen into a deep depression a long time ago.

The truth was, after all these years he still missed Alex Gallagher terribly. Yes, the old geezer had been a tough and uncompromising task master, but to Smart he was the father he never had. For some reason, Gallagher treated Smart better than the other lads, gave him more encouragement. A week before he was killed, the trainer had a private word in the lad's ear. *Son, I see greatness in you.* He told Smart if he was prepared to step up his training regime and change his attitude, Gallagher would organise a bout with the lad next in line to challenge for the Southern Area super welterweight title. If Smart could beat him, the title fight was the next step. But Gallagher's demise put paid to those plans.

He gave the bag a slight push to get it swinging. A moving target was always more challenging. He let out a scream, lined up the centre of the bag and unleashed with all his might. *Thwack.*

His scream wasn't as loud as the woman in the park, but almost.

Smart repeated the kicks, over and over, until his leg turned to jelly. He readjusted the stance, delivered another series of powerful kicks until the other leg fatigued. Enough with the Muay Thai. He reverted to boxing, conjuring up the tricky combinations of jabs, rips and hooks Gallagher had taught him. Soon his eyes stung from the sweat. Blind, he kept up the assault until the salt of tears replaced the salt of sweat.

Smart tore off the gloves and flopped into a plastic chair. He mopped away the perspiration with a towel, chugged half a litre of water.

Endorphins coursed through his body, a state of elation achieved.

Breath and core body temperature back in the normal range, Smart's elation turned to despair. His stomach turned over and over, he looked for a bucket in case the nausea turned to vomit. It passed, but the thoughts wouldn't leave him alone.

Why had he agreed to be the lookout? Now the little girl had been kidnapped. *He was an accomplice, for fuck's sake.* He'd seen on the news about the death of the ice-cream man. If the voice on the phone could arrange a cold-blooded murder – in a public area in broad daylight – what was to say he wouldn't do the same to the kid?

Yes, Smart despised Jack Lisbon with all his heart. He believed Lisbon had murdered his hero, Gallagher. He'd sworn to the cops he was sure Jack had done it. To see him suffer could only be a good thing, right? He'd agreed to set him up. *Him. Lisbon.* Not his innocent daughter, goddammit!

But now, what could he do? Go to the cops and admit he took part in this despicable act? Not a chance. That would be putting himself under the spotlight. All of the lads involved that day in the fight with Jack Lisbon of the London Metropolitan Police – himself, Micky Knox, Alan Arment, Tony Sabra – gave evidence at the murder inquiry. Lisbon beat up Knox real bad, so he heard. He didn't see it personally, because he was unconscious, courtesy of a savage punch to the jaw delivered by Lisbon. But by all accounts, Knox was writhing in pain on the floor. The other boys escaped injury, but still…Lisbon had overstepped the mark. Even if the Gallagher murder couldn't be pinned on Lisbon, the assault on Smart should have been followed up with an assault charge. Except Lisbon's lawyers were too good; they managed to get the prosecutor's office to accept the detective's bullshit self defense claims.

He grabbed his bag, headed for the changing room to take a hot shower before changing into his McDonald's uniform. He didn't care if people laughed at him, a 24-year-old man flipping hamburgers for a living. Plus he could look forward to the extra hundred quid for yesterday's job. Only now it would feel like dirty money. Perhaps he'd drop it in a busker's hat, give it to the old homeless woman who camped outside Peckham Rye station. Yes, that's what he'd do, to assuage his guilt.

His only company in the change room was a fat bloke who'd been coming to the gym just after opening hours for a while now. Smart greeted him with a deadpan nod. Fair play to the fellow, his hard work was paying off. Must have lost a good 20 lbs, toned up the arms, muscles starting to show in his thighs. Pasty white skin, though, like a cadaver. A bit of sunshine this summer would help.

As he reached into his sports bag for his favourite liquid soap, he noticed his mobile was blinking. The message contained a meme of a big Scotsman in a kilt with his hands around the bottom of what looked like a telegraph pole. The text under the image – *Don't be a fucking tosser.*

The jpeg file from the unknown number was accompanied by a message.

You did very well yesterday. Cargo received. Now, keep your head down or our friend McTaggart will be paying you and/or your lovely sister a visit when you least expect it. Have a nice day.

Smart resolved to do as he was told. He'd keep his head down and carry on as normal. But if anything happened to the child, he swore to himself he'd move heaven and Earth to avenge her.

Chapter Fifteen

MICKY KNOX RUBBED the sleep from his eyes. He felt a twinge of guilt about not mentioning the cameras to his houseguests, but it was an honest mistake. It was easy to forgive Lisbon for his outburst, all things considered. Knox slurped an instant coffee fortified with cream and three sugars, wiped his mouth with the back of his hand.

Today was going to be a busy day.

First task: find out everything he possibly could about Alan Arment, Tony Sabra and Elrod Smart. Next, stake out and interview them if necessary. Then, report back to Jack and discuss next steps.

He took another sip of coffee, leaned forward in the Norwegian-engineered ergonomic computer chair and logged onto his high-powered HP Z4 G4 workstation computer. Facebook and other social media seemed the logical place to start. For want of another strategy, he decided to investigate the men in alphabetical order of their last names.

Alan Arment. Facebook profile picture was the Welsh

flag: red dragon on green-and-white field. However, no photo of Arment himself. Knox recalled that the lad, a born-and-bred Londoner, took an exaggerated pride in his Welsh heritage. There were no significant public posts for the last month, but plenty before that. A holiday to France with some work colleagues, parties, drinking pints of lager in pubs and downing shots in nightclubs, the usual stuff for a man in his mid-twenties. A check on the other major platforms came up empty, except for LinkedIn, which revealed Arment had recently landed a job as a business sales executive for a global phone company. He was based at the firm's central office in Paddington.

Arment hadn't been sighted at McNair's for over three years. Knox remembered an aggressive young man, lean and tough, fearless in the ring, often to the point of recklessness. At the time of the Gallagher incident, he was one of the trainer's favourites. Arment had eagerly answered questions put by detectives and was vociferous in expressing his opinion that Lisbon deserved a life sentence for killing Gallagher. In one interview, Knox offered the same opinions to police, not because he wanted Jack to go down for the crime, but because he didn't want to appear complicit in the act. Play along to get along. *Yeah, I reckon that Lisbon pig done it*, he'd said to DI Jim Blackadder. *But I got no evidence to prove it. It's just a gut instinct, know what I mean?*

Knox couldn't remember the exact reason Arment stopped coming to the gym, although there was a vague memory of a tumultuous break-up with his long-time girlfriend. Rumour was, he'd gone off the rails for a while before seeking psychological help.

Knox jotted down Arment's work address and the bus and Tube combination to get him there.

Next, Tony Sabra. With his oily hair and thin moustache, back in the day he resembled a cartel drug lord. Sabra had also been absent from the gym for a number of years, maybe four. According to Instagram, he'd migrated to the United States early last year. He married a lab technician called Sally Galbraith and now worked as a mechanic for a trucking company. Knox recalled the lad was always tinkering around with cars, hands covered in grease and oil, so that made sense. There were almost daily snaps of him, the wife and a gurgling baby girl. His own appearance was virtually unchanged from what Knox remembered. He'd created a happy family thousands of miles away. Knox struck a line through Sabra's name. A simple working-class man like him, based overseas, would be as likely to organise or be involved in a kidnapping as Millwall winning the FA Cup this year.

Finally, Elrod Smart. Knox drew a big circle around the name. Like Knox, the lad had lived his whole life in South London, never venturing far from his home turf. From their conversations when they trained together, Knox remembered Smart saying his parents had emigrated from the tiny West African nation of The Gambia when Smart was a toddler. It was noteworthy for Knox because of the unusual presence of "the" in the nation's name.

Smart was the only one from "the incident", apart from himself and Paddy Sheehan, who still trained at McNair's. He was the one Gallagher had most wanted to propel into greatness, even more so than Sabra. Which was strange, Knox pondered, since it was clear to his contemporaries that Smart lacked both the talent and dedication to make the grade. Surely he hadn't been "grooming" Smart for some other nefarious purposes? Knox dismissed the idea. There'd never been the hint of any sexual impropriety surrounding Gallagher, of him liking boys. Most likely, the old trainer saw something in the lad no one else could. Wouldn't be the first time in sport an unlikely athlete made the big time. Most important from a profiling viewpoint, however, was the fact that Smart was the lad Jack knocked out cold in Gallagher's office. So that was, one, physical assault and, two, humiliation in front of his peers. A serious motive to want revenge if ever there was. Smart would be getting a visit at the local McDonald's in Rye Lane as soon as Knox was done with Alan Arment.

But there was another angle to Smart that needed looking into. He had a sister, Phoebe, who was quite a bit older, maybe five to eight years, and, if memory served correctly, she worked as a hairdresser. Could she possibly be friends with Jack's ex, Sarah, who worked in the beauty industry? A quick Internet search of salons in the area turned up a number of results, including public Facebook pages. He scanned them until he found the business where Jack had said his ex worked. Pharaoh's Hair and Nails. Its latest update after the home page, posted three days ago, featured a picture of a beaming Sarah Lisbon colouring a woman's fingernails. There was no one called Phoebe in any of the first dozen or so posts. He could scroll the page for hours, perhaps find her, perhaps not. There was a quicker way to resolve the issue. A phone call.

'Good morning, Pharaoh's Hair and Nails,' said a woman with far too much cheerfulness for early morning. 'Phoebe speaking. How can I help you?'

Knox hung up immediately. Question answered – she and Sarah Lisbon knew each other. And, importantly, Phoebe's ebullience told him the news of the crime mustn't have reached the salon.

But did that connection actually mean anything? Sarah had despised Jack at the time he fled the UK, and Phoebe may have felt the same after Jack had beaten up her little brother. But now, after five years had passed, what was Phoebe's attitude? Could she still bear a grudge…? Surely not enough to be involved in a kidnapping. The idea was ludicrous. Or was it?

Another phone call for clarity.

'Jack, it's me.'

'So soon, Micky? Have you found something out?'

'Sort of. Did you know Sarah worked with Phoebe?'

'Phoebe who?'

'Elrod Smart's sister.'

Knox heard a deep inhalation and a low whistle. 'No, I didn't.'

'Look, could she have hated you enough after you scruffed Elrod to…you know…'

'I've never met the woman. I know nothing about her.'

Knox tugged his lower lip. 'I just rang the salon. The Phoebe who answered the phone was all, let's say, sweet and innocent sounding. If I was to go just by that, I'd say she was totally unaware of the crime. I'm just ringing you in case you knew different about her.'

'Nope. I grant you, it's a coincidence her working alongside Sarah, but you know this manor, Micky. Everyone's interconnected somehow, ain't they?'

'Yeah, I guess you're right there.'

'I appreciate your attention to detail, though. What's next on your agenda?'

Knox explained his plan to chat to Arment and Smart, see if he could shake any information out of them. Jack wished him luck and disconnected the call.

Shot to the Heart

THE YOUNG BUSINESSMAN donned his designer sunglasses as he exited the Paddington tube station. Early Monday morning meant lots of commuters heading for their offices. Knox let himself be swept up in the human tide as it propelled him towards the phone company's HQ. He broke away from the crowd as he neared the target, took a deep breath and entered through the revolving glass doors.

The first obstacle was one he'd anticipated. Visitors couldn't simply enter and take the lift to the required floor. Swipe cards were required to get beyond the foyer to the bank of gleaming steel and glass elevators. He stood off to one side and observed as a steady flow of smartly dressed employees placed their cards on scanners, which activated the turnstile gates to open. He contemplated piggy-backing behind a random punter and sneaking through before the gate closed, but that tactic wasn't going to work in this environment. It might even earn him a slap in the face.

'Excuse me,' he said tentatively to a busy woman with sleek jet-black black hair that shone under the bright lights. Her sharp stilettos looked like they could pierce a man's throat.

'Yes?' she replied with a patient smile. 'Can I help you.'

Knox coughed into a fist then disarmed her with his best lost-boy smile. 'I was wondering if you could help me. I've got an appointment with a Mr...ah...let me see.' He pulled out a mini Spirax notepad, flicked a few pages over. 'Alan Arment. He's on the fourth floor I believe.'

'I work on the seventh floor.' The woman eyed Knox's expensive dark-blue suit with appreciation. He'd had it made by a tailor recently as a present to himself after achieving record quarterly earnings. He hadn't had occasion to wear it until now. 'But I have heard of Alan. Quite the sales dynamo, they say.' She smoothed the side of her skirt. 'Why don't you just call him yourself?'

'Good question. My phone's run out of charge.' He held out his switched-off iPhone. 'Ironic, hey? This being a phone company and all.'

'I guess it is.' She smiled warmly. She must be in PR, Knox thought. 'Follow me and we can go up in the lift together.' Knox wasn't sure, but he thought the woman was flirting with him. As if to confirm his suspicions, she went through the gate as slow as treacle, forcing him to press up close behind her. He closed his eyes as her musky-sweet perfume filled his nostrils.

Inside the lift he asked straight up for her business card, which she provided with a flourish. He'd not had the pleasure of good female company – social or intimate – for ages. Maybe he'd call her for a date. He glanced at the card. Jane Austin. He gave her a quizzical look. 'Yes. Just like the famous writer. Only she was Austen with an "E". I'm with an "I", like the car.'

'Never heard of that make.' Knox did his best not to sound dismissive. 'American?'

'Not at all. As British as you and me. Over thirty years ago the company became Rover. Which I'm sure you've heard of. I'm a distant relative of the founder of the original Austin company and…'

Ding.

'Oh,' said Jane. 'Here we are.' She gestured towards a reception desk. 'Sonia there will help you.' She shook Knox's hand and went about her day.

A quick word with the equally affable Sonia and Knox found himself sitting on a soft leather armchair flicking through the company's in-house magazine. He headed for the back page showing the company's performance over the last year. Profits were up and growing. Another item he'd have to add to the swelling investment portfolio.

'Micky?' Arment was unable to hide the surprise in his voice. 'I haven't laid eyes on you in years. To what do I owe the unexpected pleasure?'

'I'm in need of an upgrade to my communications systems. I saw your profile on LinkedIn and thought, why not? Alan's an old friend, he'll see me right.' Knox offered a friendly wink.

'Indeed I will, mate!' Arment ushered Knox into his work space, which wasn't an office, but a cubicle created by room dividers set to one side of the massive open-plan workspace. His area had the luxury of windows, although the view was a disappointment – the brick wall of the neighbouring building. He grabbed some literature from his desk. 'Come this way.'

Knox briefly spun a yarn about wanting to expand his import-export business, which necessitated all kinds of communications updates.

'I'm onto it, mate. Fancy a couple of one-time brawlers making good like this, hey?' said Arment, eyes shining. 'No one would have believed it back in the day.' Arment's battle scars comprised a busted nose from boxing and cauliflower ears from rugby, a game he used to play because of its "Welshness". Most noteworthy, the man's weight had ballooned so much in the intervening years Knox could scarcely credit the transformation.

'Still playing rugby?' said Knox.

'Absolutely. Although you won't be surprised to know I've switched from the backs to the forwards.' Arment patted his paunch. 'The extra bulk comes in handy for mauls and scrums and the like. But come on, let's talk about your corporate needs, boyo.'

Arment and Knox grabbed tea in take-away cups and a plate of Jaffa cakes from a communal kitchen before they headed to a compact meeting room. Before Knox could say anything further, his host launched into a nostalgic trip down memory lane, arms waving about with excitement. Knox could barely get a word in edgeways, apart from "ah ha" and "yes" and "that's right". When he'd exhausted that topic, Arment waxed lyrical about his new career in sales and how he was leading his team to great things. Among the bluster, he gave no hints he was up to anything remotely related to the kidnapping of Skye Lisbon. Either he was a great actor, or the guy was clean. Knox leaned toward the latter version. He glanced at his watch; an hour had already elapsed and he announced he had to go to another urgent appointment.

'Wait a minute! We haven't got down to brass tacks, like,' said Arment, eyebrows in a steep V. 'What about your business plan?'

'Oh, I'm still very keen. Tell you what, send me an email and we can work it all out that way, yeah?'

As they shook hands by the elevator, Knox decided to lob in a curly one. 'Nasty business about that ice-cream man getting killed on the common yesterday, hey?'

'What? I haven't heard about it. You're kidding, right?'

'No. It was on the news.'

'I don't watch the news. It wasn't old Jacob was it?'

'Ah, yeah. I'm sure that was his name,' said Knox, unable to hide his surprise. 'Did you know him?'

Tears formed in the corner of Arment's eyes, a stray one rolled down his chubby cheek. 'Yes. I always buy a choc ice off him when he's in the park. He's a rugby fan like me. Oh, this is horrible, horrible!' He reached in his pocket and pulled out a tissue.

Another one off the list.

SMART WAS the one to watch. It was a gut instinct, nothing scientific, pure hunch. Knox generally ran his life based on hard facts and data. There were exceptions to this rule. His decision to buy 500 Tesla shares seven years ago was based solely on an interview he saw with the company's founder on YouTube. Since then the price of the stock had skyrocketed.

Nausea rose in his throat as he entered the confines of the establishment. It was hard to credit this place called itself a "restaurant." The smell of the fries cooking in oil, the toasting buns and the patties on the grill made Knox want to puke. The incessant beeping of alerts from the kitchen was giving him a slight headache. He determined to focus on the job. Block out the smell and the noise.

The only vaguely palatable items on the menu board were the beverages. And to be on the safe side, he'd stick with bottled water. Surely there's nothing dodgy in that?

He shuffled forward behind a burly black man, his stout white wife, a regular customer if one was to judge by the eagerness with which she scanned the neon overhead menu, and their fidgety daughter. Ahead of them three single customers waited their turn, gazing at their phones and scrolling like zombies. Knox looked down and caught his breath. The kid, with her extraordinary mop of curly hair, wasn't that different from the photo he'd seen of Skye Lisbon.

'What do you want, tiger? Nuggets?' The father asked. The child looked up and Knox realised it was a boy. Not Skye. And why would it be? God knew where she was, but a public outing to a junk food outlet would hardly feature in the kidnappers' playbook.

'All right, Micky?' The enquiry as to his health was accompanied by a tap on the shoulder. Paddy Sheehan.

'Shh, keep it down.'

'Why?'

Sheehan was right. There was no reason to act anything other than normal. 'Sorry. I'm anxious, that's all. Remember the story?'

'Sure.' Sheehan quickly repeated the scenario Knox texted him. The story they were going to tell Smart, without arousing suspicion about an ulterior motive.

At the counter Knox ordered a bottle of water and Sheehan chose a big breakfast deal, whatever that was. Through the open-plan interior, Knox spied a familiar figure tipping a big bag of frozen chips into a vat of oil. He smiled at the sombre girl serving behind the counter. 'You reckon you could get the fellow over there,' he pointed at Smart, 'to come over for a word?'

'Sorry.' The girl shook her head. 'You'll have to wait until he's on a break.'

'Oh, that's annoying,' said Sheehan. 'Only we're in a bit of a hurry and it's real important.'

Top lip tucked into the corner of her bottom lip, she exhaled a puff of air that raised one side of her fringe. She turned demonstrably and yelled through cupped hands. 'Hey, Elrod, when d'ya get off?'

'Not when I'm looking at you, Debbie, that's for sure.' His response drew gales of laughter from the crew working the kitchen area and a confused frown from the girl. Smart turned back to the chip fryer, gave a metal basket a one-two shake and shuffled out of view.

A man with a severe military haircut appeared beside

the cashier. He wore a badge that said "Hank Cordia, Manager". He said in whisper, 'Is everything all right?'

'All good, Hank, my man,' said Sheehan. 'We need an urgent word with Elrod, that's all.'

'He's on a break in fifteen minutes.' Hank narrowed his eyes, *urgent* didn't cut it with the manager. 'I'll let him know you're here.'

Sitting at a window table, Knox could barely look at the assemblage of slops in front of Sheehan. Some kind of pancakes swimming in a whiter-than-white butter, a fried yellow rectangle, sachets of sauce. 'I thought you were taking your health seriously these days?'

'Yeah, I am. But when in Rome and all that…'

'I went to Rome last year for a two-week holiday and never touched pizza or pasta.'

'You're kidding me, right?'

Knox took a swig of his water, screwed the cap back on the bottle covered in condensation, and grinned. 'Of course, I'm kidding. But that was actually food as defined in the bleedin' dictionary. I can't say the same for that.' He pointed an accusing index finger at the pancakes.

'What do you two want, then?' Smart appeared from nowhere, rested his large hands on the table, cast a suspicious glance at his acquaintances.

'A proposition,' said Sheehan. 'One I'm hoping you'll agree to.'

Smart tugged off his black apron, folded it like a piece of paper and put it in a small backpack. 'Be quick. I'm meeting someone.'

'A girl?' said Knox with an upturned eyebrow.

'Yeah.' Smart's tone was flat. He blinked twice. He wasn't meeting anyone. 'So, I'll repeat my question. What do you two clowns want from me?'

'Simple, really. Me and Paddy are thinking of making a serious comeback to boxing.' Knox felt a sharp nudge in the thigh from Sheehan. First mistake.

'Fuck off! Paddy's already back in the game. What do you take me for?'

Quick, recover it. 'Yeah, everyone knows that. You didn't pick up on the key thing I said. He wants to get *serious*. He's still young enough to go from a scrapper to a title contender. And so am I. I'm doing OK in business, but I miss the thrill of the ring. I'm all fired up and ready to kick some arse.'

'What he said.' Sheehan nodded furiously. 'And as for me, my three bouts for the entire last year is hardly a career, innit?'

Smart shook his head. 'Every mug with a pair of boxing gloves thinks they're a world beater. I thought the same.' His long arm swept in an arc. 'But this is reality. Now, if you don't mind, I've got better things to do.'

A hand darted out and stayed Smart's hand. Sheehan said, voice almost breathy with mock desperation, 'Smarty, c'mon man. This is a golden opportunity for you. Micky here's going to pay you to help us.'

Knox noted a twitch in Smart's eye. 'How much?'

'Well.' Knox wriggled his backside into the hard plastic bench seat. 'That depends on your level of commitment.'

Ten minutes later, and Smart was sitting next to Knox in the booth and fully on board with the scheme, at least in theory. Sheehan, in particular, softened him up with inflated praise. *You've got the best left jab in the business, Smarty. You sure can take a punch. Who knows? If you step up, you'll be chasing titles yourself.* After fifteen minutes, the burger flipper was agog with excitement at the prosect of earning £50 per session by offering himself up as a sparring partner. The sessions would be virtually no-holds-barred affairs, almost simulating real fights. The man's eagerness to participate told Knox one thing: there was no way Smart was expecting a big pay day from the ransom. Otherwise their meagre cash incentive would have had no appeal.

'So we're agreed, then?' said Knox. 'I'll work out a schedule and let you know. Give me your phone number and I'll text you when it's all worked out.'

Although encouraging in terms of ruling him out as a bad guy, Smart's behaviour didn't guarantee he wasn't involved in the kidnapping. Knox tried the same line he'd used on Arment. No sooner were the words "ice-cream man" out of his mouth than Smart had knocked over the bottle of water, gathered his apron and backpack and stood up. He offered some incoherent excuses and rushed out the door.

Back out on the street, Sheehan said, 'What now?'

'He knows something, all right.'

'You think he suspects we're working for Jack?'

'Highly doubtful. He was there in the interview room when I told the cops I wanted Lisbon to get a life sentence for killing Gallagher. And you practically hypnotised him with all that smoke you were blowing up his arse. Which, by the way, proved extremely useful.'

'How?'

Knox pulled out his mobile, showed Sheehan an app he'd installed. 'While you were buttering him up I slipped a tiny tracking device into his backpack. Let's see where he goes and what he does.'

Chapter Sixteen

THE GREY URBAN sprawl of London, Birmingham and their satellite towns and conurbations gave way to grand old oaks, elms and maples, here and there stretching limbs created dappled shade above country lanes. Under an almost cloudless sky, inhabitants of serene villages going about their quiet lives turned on the spot and blinked hard as Lex Buskin's red Jaguar whooshed past. Speed limits all but ignored, the sports car tore past thatched cottages and sandstone pubs, churches and souvenir shops, parks and gardens filled with budding flowers and bulbs. Vibrant hyacinths, jonquils, tulips, daffodils. Jack stared open-mouthed at the calming bucolic scenery, strangely foreign to a man long absent, now back on home soil.

'What's the ETA on our arrival at Cedric's office?' Jack mashed spearmint gum in aching jaws. 'Seems to be taking forever.' Jack had changed his mind about running things tucked away inside the safehouse. His nervous system simply couldn't allow him to be the hands-off "Charlie" with his "angels" running around doing the groundwork.

'Soon, mate. You probably noticed I've been exceeding the speed limit the whole bleedin' way, except for when Lucy tells me there's a–'

As if on cue, the Navigator system's assured female voice warned: *Speed camera ahead.* Bruiser eased off the accelerator, bringing the car to two miles an hour under the limit.

'I know, and thanks. It's just that time's marching on, innit?' Jack tapped the dash clock. 'After this we've got another epic drive ahead of us. We can't waste a second, sunshine!'

Bruiser flashed Jack a smile of understanding, quickly refocussed on the road as the carriageway narrowed. Soon, the landscape shifted to urban again as the A5 motorway led them to the outskirts of Shrewsbury, the administrative centre of the county of Shropshire. They approached a bend with oncoming traffic shielded by a dry stone wall, making Bruiser slow down again. Within minutes they were on the doorstep to the town: a right into London Road, across the river Severn, and they'd arrived in Shrewsbury.

'An interesting fact. Charles Darwin was born here,' said Bruiser, eyes peeled as he steered along ever tightening streets.

'Is that right? It doesn't look like much has evolved here since that time,' observed Jack.

'Good one, mate. I don't know how you can maintain your wits at a time like this.'

'It ain't easy, lemme tell you.' Jack watched people dawdling with shopping bags, strolling about like they hadn't a care in the world. 'There's so much racing through my head I can barely keep it together. I mean, Skye could be anywhere, they could be keeping her in appalling conditions.' Jack's fists bunched involuntarily by his thighs. 'It's the not knowing that's doing my head in, know what I mean?'

Bruiser nodded slowly, reached across with his left hand and gave Jack's hand a comradely squeeze. 'I've got no kids myself, mate. Just a pet goldfish to care for. So I'm not going to be one of those people who says they understand what you're going through, because I can't. But I'll do whatever it takes to help you get Skye home, OK?

'Cheers, pal. Appreciated.'

Fifteen minutes of negotiating the tricky system of one-way streets in the town centre and they'd found Cedric Gallagher's architect practice, located on the picturesque Victoria Quay. The office sat on the second floor of a quaint red brick building overlooking the river, outdoor dining cafes with a sprinkling of customers, and a gateway to the departure jetty for river cruises. Jack pointed across the steering wheel 'Park over there.'

'What? You're kidding. We'll never fit.'

'Rubbish. Squeeze through the bollards and park under the willow trees.'

Bruiser edged the car forward at a snail's pace; there was barely a millimetre of clearance between two bollards. He killed the engine and applied the handbrake. 'I was risking the duco there. Now, are you ready?'

'Give me a moment.' Jack reached into the back seat and retrieved a bright orange Sainsbury's tote bag. He retrieved the items that comprised the makeshift disguise. He donned a brunette wig and topped it with a hunter-green beret. Ultra-dark sunglasses completed the ensemble. He twisted the rear vision mirror and checked himself out. Not even DC Claudia Taylor would recognise him.

'You look a right wally.' Bruiser grinned with appreciation.

'Thanks.' Jack's phone buzzed in his pants pocket.
'What is it?'
'Update from Knox. Listen. We're tailing Elrod Smart. He couldn't get away quick enough when I brought up the subject of the dead ice-cream man. Alan Arment, on the other hand, burst into tears when he heard the same news. I'd say scratch Arment as a suspect. Elrod's a different matter. He knows more than he's letting on. I'll text with any developments. Holy shit, Bruiser! This could be critical if Smart's involved. I knocked him out cold four years ago, humiliated him in front of his peers. He could harbour a massive grudge.'

'There's nothing you can do about it now. Let Knox and Sheehan do their thing. Maybe the answer lies here in Shrewsbury and not in London at all.'

'You're right. Dammit, this walking on egg shells is so frustrating. C'mon, let's rattle Gallagher junior.'

'YOU'RE lucky Mr Gallagher's in today. There was supposed to be an important county council meeting but it was cancelled at the last minute.' The dowdy secretary sporting a perm whose use-by date expired in 1985 reached for the phone. 'One moment.' She buzzed her employer. 'OK, thanks.' She eyeballed the two men. 'He'll see you now.'

Cedric Gallagher stood, did up the top button of his light-grey jacket, and greeted his guests with warm two-handed handshakes and an eager smile.

Jack caught his breath for a moment. Cedric Gallagher had inherited his late father's features; he was almost a younger version of the man. A clone. Even the hairstyle – wavy and just above the shoulder, was the same. It was like Jack was staring into his deeply troubled past. Then he realised, there was a subtle difference – unlike dad, Cedric hadn't spent his youth getting punched in his pretty little head so his features were intact. He probably had all his own teeth. In other ways, despite the physical resemblance, the son was the antithesis of the father. A framed architecture degree from Cardiff University hung proudly behind Cedric's luxurious white-leather office chair. Alex Gallagher didn't finish high school. Cedric was a member of the Conservative Party, Alex had been Labour to the core. Cedric was alive, Alex was dead.

Jack quickly pulled himself together, offered his own beaming smile. After exchanging pleasantries, the architect organised brewed coffee with bottles of sparkling mineral water as chasers. Jack slipped into a mini euphoria as the super-strong brew worked its way through his veins. Playing this charade wasn't going to be easy, but he and Bruiser hadn't been able to think of a better idea at short notice. If they pulled it off, Cedric would be unable to hide his guilt if he was involved.

'Please, Jake and Les. Take a seat. Tell me about your grand plans to build a house in our delightful county. Moving here would be the best decision you ever made.'

For the next ten minutes Jack lied without pause or hesitation, like he was reading from a movie script, in a Liverpool accent he'd managed to master after years of practice. It was so good he'd occasionally fooled actual Liverpudlians. He'd had plenty of time to rehearse the role on the long drive from London. He and Bruiser, aka Jake Lenton and Les Brown, were a gay couple living in inner London, looking to escape to the country. They had plenty of money to spend and wanted a house they could call their own. They'd heard Cedric was the best architect in the county, perhaps in all of England, and they were eager to secure his services. They'd agreed Jack would do all the talking.

'What style of house are you leaning towards?' Cedric asked once Jack had finished describing their situation.

Jack aka Jake admitted he liked modern, Scandinavian designs with open floor plans, whereas his partner Les preferred traditional English homes with low ceilings to bump your head on and pokey little rooms – they all laughed – and that undefinable element, character. They were prepared to demolish pre-existing structures if they found the right property.

'So,' said Cedric. 'Would a blend of old and new perhaps work for you? We've designed a number of such houses in the last few years, where we employ modern concepts and materials with older ones such as recycled timbers, bricks and sandstone. We even build moats with drawbridges! How old-fashioned can you get?'

Jack and Bruiser chuckled along with Cedric, who was now slipping into salesman mode.

'Here, have a flick through our prospectus. I'm sure you'll find inspiration from some of our award-winning projects.' Cedric grabbed a couple of large-format brochures from a drawer in a file cabinet, handed one each to Jack and Bruiser. The pair feigned keen interest in the sketches and brightly coloured computer graphics. Bruiser acted way too camp for Jack's liking, pointed at random designs, even giggled and clapped his hands like a child at a birthday party. Jack rubbed his chin thoughtfully, as if seriously contemplating this or that house.

Jack had to admit to himself, one of those concrete-and-steel bad boys would look a treat by the Bousted River back in Yorkville, Australia. A place he and Skye could...*Enough time wasting Lisbon, get on with it.*

'To be honest,' said Jack. 'We want something that's got one feature at the front of your mind when you're designing our home, something that outweighs everything else.'

A quizzical look instantly transformed Cedric's face into that of his father four years ago, in total shock seconds after Jack plunged a razor-sharp letter opener into the man's neck. Jack readjusted the large pair of sunglasses and tugged on the beret as his heart began to gallop. *What if this bloke recognises me?* They'd never met in person, but Cedric must have seen lots of photos of Jack.

'What feature is that?' said Cedric. 'A pool or a conservatory? Something grander?'

'Safety,' said Jack. 'We've got a little boy.'

'Oh, how sweet!' said Cedric, flashing an avuncular smile. 'I'm sure the two of you are perfect parents. More coffee?'

'No thanks,' said Jack as Bruiser pushed his fine-china cup into the centre of the table. 'Oh, OK then. As I was saying, safety's our priority. We fear for our little Oliver's wellbeing all the time. Always bumping into things and hurting himself, he is. It's driving us crazy, isn't is darling?'

Bruiser kept stirring sugar into his coffee. Jack cleared his throat. 'I said we…

'Oh, yes, dear,' said Bruiser. 'He's a devil, that one!'

'Ok…' said Cedric doubtfully. Was he smelling a rat, Jack wondered. 'We always try and incorporate our clients' wishes. What specifically did you have in mind? Rounded edges everywhere, perhaps?'

'We'd like…ah…' Jack saw tiny stars flickering before his eyes, blinking on and off for a moment, and then whizzing around and around in random patterns. A sharp pain gripped his left side just behind the middle rib. *What gives? Am I having a heart attack?* He was aware of Bruiser and

Gallagher talking, fussing over him, easing him across the room and onto a soft couch. Someone sat him upright, pushed his head between his knees. 'Breathe in and out, sweetheart. Nice and steady.' It was Bruiser. Jack did as he was told, took a massive deep breath, exhaled. He sat up straight, head bowed slightly. The hard rim of a bottle touched his lips. He eagerly gulped down the mineral water. He sensed his hands were shaking like he had Parkinson's disease... *What's happening?* 'He climbs over everything, forever falling and hurting himself, we have to protect him at all costs.' He heard himself whisper the words. Jack, hazy as his thinking was, continued the agreed narrative, stayed in character. In the recesses of his memory, he recalled Sarah and himself had seriously worried about Skye's overly adventurous nature when she was a toddler, about the possibility she could do real damage to herself. The kid had no fear. He blinked hard, three times. The pain had gone, his breathing was almost regular again. The episode was over.

'Shall we continue this at another time?' said Cedric. 'I'm sure we can take care of your needs. I've got a son, myself. Your kids are the most important things in your life, I understand that. My dad was like you in a way.'

Jack's ears pricked up. *Here we go.*

'Your dad must've been a wonderful bloke.' A heart-to-heart with the son of the man Jack had killed. Only now did Jack wonder how it was that Cedric wasn't even slightly suspicious of what was going on here. *It's because he's not involved.*

'Indeed he was. Snatched away from his family by a murderer.'

'How horrible!' said Jack, sweat building behind his neck. 'Did they catch whoever did it?'

'No. The killer is still at large and it's a disgrace.' Cedric fetched a crystal decanter from a liquor cabinet, gestured towards glasses on a tray and raised his eyebrows.

'Ah, no thanks,' said Jack.

'Me either,' said Bruiser.

'The police know who did it, but they failed in bringing the culprit to justice.'

'Wow,' said Jack, wishing he could drink half of that decanter of whisky. But now was definitely not the time to relapse. 'You must be filled with thoughts of vengeance. I know I would be.'

'Actually, Jake, no. I used to want the bastard strung up from a gallows. But five years have elapsed, and I'm sure whoever did it – and I know who did it – is suffering from guilt.'

Not likely sunshine. Your father deserved what he got. That's what Jack wanted to say. Instead: 'That's very…forgiving of you. If it were my family member murdered, I'd pursue the matter to the bitter end. To get justice.'

Cedric pointed to something Jack hadn't noticed, or he had seen it and not attached any significance to it. A small silver crucifix hanging on the wall to the right of Cedric's framed university degree. 'I'm a born again Christian, Jake. Forgiveness is the only way forward. If I hadn't found Jesus, I'd still be gripped with hatred. Like my sister still is. Consumed with it, if I'm to be honest. She just can't move on.'

'Let's say a prayer for your father, shall we?' said Jack, adrenaline threatening to tip him over the edge again.

Cedric muttered a few holy sounding words with his eyes closed.

'Thank you, Cedric, that was very touching. I don't know about you, Les, but I'm overwhelmed with emotion.'

Jack turned to Cedric. 'Perhaps we could come back another time?'

'Sure.' Cedric tipped the contents of the glass down his neck. 'I think I'll shut up shop early today.'

———

JACK WAITED until they'd crossed the historic English Bridge before removing his disguise. The wig has started to make his scalp itch. 'I want to catch Gallagher's daughter Alicia before close of business. How long does it take to drive to Ipswich from here?'

Bruiser leaned forward in his seat, pressed some buttons on the dash to set the course. 'Computer says three and a half hours.'

'Can you get there before 6:00pm?'

'Only if I speed even more than before and we don't stop for toilet breaks.'

'Step on it, sunshine. I need you to make a phone call along the way. I'll tell you what to say.'

———

THE TRAFFIC FLOWED FREELY on the A14 motorway for most of the trip. On the outskirts of the town of Bury St Edmonds, however, it slowed to an agonisingly slow crawl before coming to a complete standstill. The warm moisture behind Jack's neck began to soak into his collar, his armpits were wet. Their plan was ruined. Bruiser had rung and made the appointment, but now there was no way they'd arrive in time to catch Alicia Rafter née Gallagher at her dental practice.

'Damn this.' Jack glanced at his watch. 'It's already

5:15pm. How long does your navigator say it takes to drive to Ipswich from where we are now?'

'With or without a traffic jam to contend with?'

'Without, you moron!'

'Oi, no need for name calling.'

'Sorry, mate.' Jack forced the contrition, not easy when the man had asked such a stupid question, even if in jest. 'The stress is getting to me.'

'Apology accepted. Wait a second, let me see what we're dealing with.' Bruiser fiddled with the settings on his GPS. 'Satellite data says there's a big hold up maybe a quarter of a mile ahead of us. The traffic divider rail means we can't turn back and take an alternate route. Normally it would take, lemme see, another thirty-three minutes from here to Alicia's work. But with this…we're going to have to wait, I guess.' Bruiser shrugged.

'Fuck this for a joke! I don't want you to be confronting the woman at her own house. People are always more defensive at home. Sitting here is sending my blood pressure through the roof. I've got an idea. Let me in the driver's seat, will ya?'

'Why?'

Jack was already out of the car and making his way to the other side. Positions swapped, Jack did up his seat belt and eased the Jaguar between the two east-bound lanes but the gap was too narrow to allow the car to squeeze through.

'What the hell are you doing? We're stuck fast, mate. There's no getting through there.'

Without replying, Jack pushed on the horn pad in the middle of the steering wheel while simultaneously flicking the high beams on and off. Bright light reflected off the boot of the cars immediately in front, heads in vehicles turned to see where the blaring ruckus was coming from.

Bruiser gasped as a slight gap opened, then widened enough for them to bisect the two lanes. 'What the…?'

Jack grinned. 'It's amazing what a bit of throwing your weight around can do.'

Vehicles continued to separate like a giant zipper undoing. They negotiated a slight bend in the motorway when the cause of the holdup became apparent. A messy mangle of metal and shattered glass across the carriageway – an accident involving two small sedans and a delivery truck. Attending the scene were ambulances, police cars and motorcycles. First responders in high-viz gear scurried about, pushing gurneys, comforting people, taking photographs with huge cameras. A constable looked up and shot a disapproving glare at the approaching Jaguar.

'Shit,' said Bruiser. 'We're in trouble now.'

'Maybe not.'

The uniform gestured for them to stop. Jack stopped pressing the horn, wound down his window. 'You have to let us through, officer.' Jack summoned his most authoritative tone. 'It's extremely urgent.'

'You must be joking.' The cop was incredulous. 'We've got a serious accident here. It's hard enough looking after the injured and managing traffic without idiots like you making life harder. I'm going to book you with being a public nuisance and erratic driving.' The man reached into his pocket and pulled out a notebook. 'Right, ID please.'

Jack handed over a laminated card. The policeman turned it over in his hand, reading both sides.

'Australian license, hey? So you think you're Crocodile Dundee or something, hey? Laws don't apply to your type, do they? And…hang on a minute…' Jack's smile broadened as the young constable's features began to twitch. 'Are you…

are you the same Detective Jack Lisbon who migrated to Australia and solved all those murders?'

'One and the same, sunshine. I'm working with MI6 on a huge international case right now, and this delay ain't helping matters. So, if you don't mind…'

The constable handed back Jack's license. 'I'm so sorry for calling you an idiot.'

'Not a problem. I'd have thought the same if I were in your shoes. Only doing your job.'

'Would you like an escort to wherever it is you're going?'

Jack touched a forefinger to the side of his nose. 'It's a hush-hush operation, so that won't be necessary. Tell you what, if you could hop on your motorcycle and see us through to the other side of the accident, that'd be much appreciated. And please, whatever you do, don't mention having seen me. It could compromise our undercover status if word got out, understood?'

'Understood.' The constable gave a mini salute, jumped on a blue-and-white BMW motorbike and shepherded Jack and Bruiser past the crash scene.

'I really like your car,' said Jack. 'Mind if I drive the rest of the way?'

'Be my guest,' said Bruiser, shaking his head.

JACK PARKED the Jag in a tree-lined side street two blocks from Alicia Rafter's dental practice. The frightful wig and beret back on, he gave Bruiser some last minute instructions. While Bruiser was carrying out the job, Jack would lay low in the car.

'You sure you're up for this?' said Jack, looking nervously from side to side and over his shoulder.

Bruiser nodded confidently before touching Jack lightly on the shoulder. 'I'm ready.' He strode the 300 metres to the front door of the dental practice. The brass plaques advised there were two other dentists working here in addition to the target. Bruiser took out his phone, found the voice recorder app and turned it on. He was sure he'd be able to recall the important details and report back to Jack accurately, but Lisbon wasn't taking any chances. The omission of vital information could prove costly.

Inside the cosy reception area, from behind a glass partition an early-twenties female in big nerdy glasses looked up from her computer. 'I'm sorry, sir. We're about to close for the day.'

'Yes, I know. I made an appointment to see Ms Rafter at 6:00pm.'

The woman cocked an eyebrow. 'That's impossible. The last appointment with *Doctor* Rafter was thirty minutes ago.'

Bruiser laughed uneasily. Why did he say Ms? 'Not that kind of appointment. My teeth are fine, see?' He pulled back his lips and bared his teeth like a chimpanzee, then instantly regretted it. This undercover work was wrecking his nerves. 'I called her on her mobile. It's regarding a personal matter.'

'Uh, right,' the woman said warily. 'Just let me confirm. Your name?'

'Briggs. Leo Briggs. I'm a private investigator from London.' He held out a business card then quickly put it back in his wallet before she had a chance to read it.

The woman picked up a telephone receiver, relayed the information. 'You *are* expecting him? OK, fine.' She replaced the receiver, stared daggers at Bruiser. 'She'll meet you in the waiting area in five minutes. Please take a seat.'

Bruiser walked to a side room, sat on a hard plastic

chair. He leafed through some well-thumbed five-year-old Readers Digests, not taking in a single word as the text blurred on the page. Bruiser had been less jittery watching the stock exchange crash in 2008. Taking in the minimalistic surroundings, it struck him that being an architect in Shrewsbury must pay better than being a dentist in Ipswich. Either that, or the late Alex Gallagher's daughter was less pretentious than the son.

A cough made Bruiser jump in his seat. 'You said you've got a new lead on my father's murder?'

Bruiser stood, extended his hand to the woman in the light blue scrubs. 'Yes I have.'

'Great news, wonderful news in fact. Is it that bastard Lisbon? You've finally got proof?'

'Well, I…'

'Can you wait five minutes while I get changed?' She dropped her voice to a whisper. 'I'd rather discuss this away from inquisitive ears.' She gestured with her head towards the receptionist hidden behind a wall. 'She's a wonder at organising things, but a frightful gossip. There's a quiet little café around the corner. OK with you?'

With no options, Bruiser simply nodded.

The café appointment had progressed precisely five minutes and twenty-seven seconds when it suddenly ceased to be necessary. No sooner had they ordered a pot of Earl Grey tea accompanied with scones, raspberry jam and clotted cream than Alicia posed a question that immediately eliminated her from suspicion without Bruiser having to do any probing at all.

'So,' said Alicia Rafter, five years' worth of bitterness and anger turning her courteous smile into an ugly scowl. 'When do you think the police will be extraditing that fucker Lisbon from Australia?'

Chapter Seventeen

THE TRAFFIC THICKENED the closer they got to St Albans. On the plus side, Jack had never driven a civilian car this fancy and powerful. Even when the line of vehicles slowed to a trickle along stretches of the M25 which skirted London to the north, the luxury inside made it bearable. A hard-core country music fan, Bruiser didn't argue when Jack selected a classical radio. Jack was leaning forward to increase the volume of Mozart's Clarinet Concerto in A major when a call came through on Lex Buskin's phone. DCI Lars Pedersen, asking for Jack.

'Put him on loudspeaker, Bruiser.' Jack stared into the back of an 18-wheeler transporting a cargo of Dutch beer. 'Better if we both hear it.'

'Did you have any luck with the Gallagher children?' said Pedersen.

'Negative, Lars,' said Jack. He explained the reasons Cedric and Alicia were now scratched as potential suspects.

'No way you were rumbled by either of them?'

'No chance,' chimed in Bruiser. 'Alicia never clapped

eyes on him. And Cedric was clueless. Have you heard Jack do a Scouse accent while playing the part of a gay man?'

'Ah, no.'

'Enough of that.' Jack slapped the indicator and overtook a pensioner in an ancient Morris Minor, chin on his steering wheel and terror in his eyes. 'The point is, we're no closer to discovering who snatched my...' Jack bit his knuckle. At times he thought this was all a game, and he was dreaming, then the brutal reality hit home. Some prick had kidnapped his daughter.

'Don't be disheartened,' said Pedersen. 'Eliminating suspects means the chance of others being guilty increases.'

As they pulled into the driveway of the St Albans safehouse, Jack noticed a curious neighbour peering between the slats of venetian blinds. Just a pair of dark eyes, still – unsettling. 'Any news on the CCTV from the gym?'

'Yes, we got the footage for Saturday. I sent a PC around to fetch it. The manager was most cooperative. Upshot is, the cameras captured our man McTaggart from several angles as he made his way around the gym. Some action of him sparring and chatting to other patrons. Quite a handsome chap for a thug.'

'Can I see it?'

'Absolutely.' Pedersen undertook to place the large MP4 file on a file sharing website, gave Jack a web address and passcode to access it.

'Thanks. Is he a known person?' Jack held his breath.

'Not on our UK databases, which are comprehensive. And I've got access to the most sophisticated face recognition software in the world. I could share the footage with the FBI and other sister agencies, but again, that's going to require more red tape. Plus there's the time factor.'

Jack chewed a fingernail. 'Damn it. Is there no way you can do that on the quiet?'

'Absolutely not. Out of the question. Unless, of course, you make an official request and we hand the case over to the Anti Kidnap and Extortion Unit. Then all manner of procedures can be expedited.'

'No! I'm not risking it. I've basically got 24 hours until we make the Bitcoin transaction. Tell you what, if we can't figure out who's got her and where she is by lunchtime tomorrow, I'll relent.'

'Promise?'

'On the proviso you swear not to do anything that might tip off the perps before the payment deadline.'

A sigh of relief from Pedersen. 'That's a good lad.'

Chapter Eighteen

JACK AND BRUISER hunched around the screen of the laptop Bruiser had brought to St Albans. A bigger screen would have been better, but, Jack told himself, there was no point dreaming about what you can't have. The relevant sections of the medium-resolution video played out for the second time. Pedersen had used a sophisticated editing tool to find and bookmark only those sections where McTaggart was on camera, otherwise it would take a day to view the entire contents at normal speed.

'Did you see him that day yourself?' Jack reached for a glass of water. His eyelids were leaden, mouth dry despite the constant rehydration. Perhaps it was coffee counteracting the hydrating effect of the H_2O.

'Yeah, but I paid little attention at the time. None, if I'm going to be honest.'

'Hmm.' Jack drummed his fingers on the table top. 'He is a unit, as they say. Hard to miss. Looks a bit like the Scots bloke in that time travel drama all the women are crazy for. What's his name?

'Jamie Fraser.'

'Didn't expect you to be up on those women's shows.'

'Oi. Normal blokes like it too!'

'Sure they do.' Jack cracked his knuckles. 'So, shall we go through it again?' He shot Bruiser a hopeful look. 'Once more for luck?'

Bruiser let out an exasperated breath. 'And what new stuff are we going to see? Nothing. It's already after midnight.'

'I've got an idea. We need some context with this.'

'Meaning?'

'I'm not sure. There's two hour's worth of footage showing McTaggart, right?'

'Yeah.' Bruiser consulted an onscreen summary document Pedersen had sent to accompany the video. 'A whisker under. One hundred and eighteen minutes to be exact. And we've seen it all. Twice!'

'And how many bookmarks are there?'

'Ah, eight. One where he enters the building, one for the short sparring session where he clobbers poor Johnny Hannan, five corresponding to chats he had with clients, two of them being Knox and Sheehan, and one of him exiting the premises.'

'Right.' Jack worked a wad of gum overtime. 'And it's clear from the video that none of the lads he spoke to were handing out information willy-nilly. Especially Hannan, who needs to pay more attention to his guard if he wants to avoid getting his face rearranged.'

Bruiser tapped a pen on the side of his coffee mug. 'I agree. Each one was clearly shaking his head when McTaggart spoke to them. If body language is anything to go by, they gave nothing away.'

'We have to cast the net wider.'

'Explain.'

'Let's have a look at what's happening five minutes either side of the bookmarks.'

'And what's that going to do?'

Jack's deadpan face stared at Bruiser. 'Buggered if I know. It's another eighty minutes all up, maybe we'll catch a glimpse of something. You can go to bed if you like. I'm not going to sleep until I've got Skye back in my arms.'

Bruiser patted Jack on the shoulder. 'As if I'd abandon you, mate.' He fussed about in the kitchen for a couple of minutes and returned with a pot of piping-hot percolated coffee.

'I'm glad we did that,' said Jack as the video came to an end.

Bruiser leaned back in his chair, arms folded. 'You are?'

'Yep.'

'Well, I must've missed it.'

'Are you kidding?'

Jack rewound the footage. 'One more look, OK?'

'If you insist.'

Jack's finger hovered over the mouse ready to click when his burner phone burst into life with its quaint analogue ringtone. The +61 country code meant it could only be Claudia Taylor calling from Australia. 'Sorry, Bruiser, I gotta take this.'

Buskin nodded his understanding, headed for the bathroom. The man had a bladder like a zeppelin, Jack reflected. He could put away gallons of fluid but rarely went for a tip out.

'Did you find anything useful?' said Jack. He stood, began to pace the floor of the kitchen.

'Depends what you call useful.'

'Anything that'll help me find Skye.'

'What will help you find her is calling in the experts.'

There was nothing worse than going over old ground, even with a respected colleague. He counted to ten in his head. He then calmly explained he'd made the decision to hand the matter over to DCI Pedersen if Jack himself failed to uncover the perpetrators' identity. Pedersen would coordinate with the Anti Kidnap and Extortion Unit while Jack bit his nails and quietly lost his mind with worry.

'OK,' said Claudia. 'I'm proud of you. Anyway, here's what I found out. The gym is currently owned by someone called John Thomas Smith. At least I assume he's the owner, but on the official record he's down as the one and only PSC, or Person with Significant Control.'

'Got any contact details?'

'Kind of. There's a so-called registered office address for the company, JT Smith Ltd. A post office box in Luton, wherever that is. That's also the service address of Mr Smith. About the only thing I can tell you about him is he's a citizen of the United Kingdom.'

'A phone number?'

'Sorry, no.' She paused a moment. Jack heard the sound of a kettle's whistle. It was early morning in Yorkville. She'd be preparing her favourite Earl Grey. 'Why don't you simply ask the manager? Surely they'll know who owns the place.'

'I don't want to alarm people with nosey questions. I might inadvertently tip off the wrong people.'

'Fair enough. I also investigated Gallagher's widow. Seems she's living the high life in Italy with her much younger man. Gets herself into the fashion pages. Looks like she's had a ton of plastic surgery.'

Jack rubbed his forehead. Her searches hadn't turned up anything positive to go on. 'What about the coppers whose names I gave you?'

Claudia confirmed what he'd already learned about Keogh, Blackadder, Keddie and Dreyfuss.

'So that's it?' said Jack.

Bruiser shuffled back from the bathroom, gave Jack a wink as if to say *carry on with your conversation, don't mind me*.

'Yes,' said Taylor. 'I...ah... I guess what I really want to say is this – I think whoever took Skye could be an opportunist, someone you haven't even considered, someone who isn't on Bruiser's list. And that's why–'

'Yes! I know what you're going to say. And I will authorise them to act. Tomorrow.'

'Good luck, Jack. I'll be praying for you.' Claudia disconnected the call.

'Ready?' said Jack, retaking his seat and looking across to Bruiser. Before the man could reply Jack restarted the video then stopped it thirty seconds before the last bookmark. 'There.'

'What?'

'Look harder, for pity's sake. You can see him just behind that group of women leaving the gym.'

'Where?'

'There, there!' Jack stopped the video and stabbed at the screen with a shaking forefinger.

'Geez, Jack. You're right. It's him!'

Chapter Nineteen

SHE COULDN'T OPEN the window, it was jammed shut. So she rested her dimpled chin on the windowsill and stared into the open space outside. A vast cobalt sea stretched to a point where it imperceptibly changed colour and melded with the horizon. Dark clouds and water became one indistinguishable greyness. Before the raging waves perched low cliffs that overlooked a crescent coastline, yellowy-white sand curving softly towards the end of a bluff. Between the building she was being held in and the edge of the cliffs sprawled lush green meadows dotted with black-faced sheep, huddling under one of only a handful of trees on the acreage. In another fenced-off paddock, a dozen or so long-haired cattle grazed. Their shaggy coats reminded her of Oswald, the teddy bear Mum bought at a flea market in Brixton when Skye was three. Out there, beyond her prison, was a landscape so unlike the concrete urban environment Skye knew, the only environment she had ever known in her short ten years. Out there was the most beautiful and terrifying place she'd ever seen.

But where was she?

Skye reasoned she was probably on the second floor of a farmhouse. The exposed brick, the cold, cold air, the smell of straw and animals that seemed to cling to the walls. But where was the farmhouse? It could be anywhere, another country even. And who else was here? If she had her dad's detective brains, she'd be able to piece it all together in a flash.

Another peek outside. Maybe there were some clues. Immediately below the window ran a narrow gravel driveway, in which was parked a shiny black car and a white van. She had a vague recollection of being carried over someone's shoulder, looking up and seeing the van. But she'd been disoriented when they brought her here, as well as worn out from struggling and screaming under the gag, so it could have been another vehicle. The last thing she remembered clearly was being at the park in South London, her father running to help a woman in distress. But why had someone knocked Skye out and taken her away from her dad? It didn't make sense.

She looked out the window again, scanned the sea for a ship, a boat, any sign of human life. Nothing. Just relentless, surging, white-capped waves and seagulls hovering around the rim of the cliff face. A shaft of sunlight penetrated the thick clouds for a moment before the hole in the heavens closed and a gloomy, grey dusk settled in. A soft slanting rain began to tap at the window.

She tip-toed to the door, wooden and heavy, pressed an ear to it and listened as hard as she could. A murmur of voices from somewhere. A couple of men, it sounded like, maybe a whole gang of them. Then a burst of laughter. What was so funny? She tried the handle again. Locked, just like before.

Another scream might get their attention. She cupped her hands around her lips and hollered with all her might. Not a word, like HELP, but a primal scream from the gut. A howl of protest.

Oh dear, that hurt. She wouldn't do it again. Her throat was red raw from fits of yelling and screaming over the last hour. But what else could she do?

The room was bare except for the manky old single bed covered with a stained cotton sheet and a prickly woollen blanket. She grabbed the blanket and wrapped it around her shoulders, the bone-chilling cold made her teeth chatter. A touch of the radiator, hoping for a semblance of warmth but feeling none. There was no other furniture or decorations, nor any hard object to throw and perhaps break the window. She decided to check in the freezing ensuite bathroom again. Unlikely, but maybe she'd missed something she could use to help her escape. A peek in the cupboards – empty. There was a roll of toilet paper on the floor, a couple of towels and a bar of soap. Not even a toothbrush to hack at the door with. And no toilet brush. What sort of dirty, disgusting people lived in this house? Mum would be appalled at that oversight. She was overcome by a desperate thirst, a dryness in the mouth, but there were no cups. She turned on the tap, craned her neck and guzzled the stream of fresh, ice-cold water.

Wiping her mouth with the back of her hand, Skye started to realise, things were looking pretty bad. She heard and felt a grumbling in her tummy. Not famished, but getting close. The last thing she'd eaten was a choc ice. Would she starve to death in this room? And worst of all, apart from staring out the window, there was nothing to occupy her mind. No mobile phone to play games on, not a book or magazine to read, no TV to watch. The grey clouds were blotting out more and more light by the minute – soon she wouldn't be able to see the ocean through the window.

Skye sat on the edge of the bed, put her head in her hands and started to cry.

Where was Daddy?

All cried out, she curled up in the foetal position. Darkness was now complete and, despite shivering with cold, Skye fell into a deep sleep.

Chapter Twenty

IT WAS LATER than he had stayed up in years. The ongoing success of his business required adequate sleep. Tonight, that good habit had been kicked to the kerb.

At 01:07 hours on a workday Tuesday, Micky Knox and Paddy Sheehan were sitting around the small kitchen table in Knox's flat, watching nineties grunge music videos online. Despite the urge to turn the sound up, Knox kept the volume at a level that wouldn't disturb neighbours in the apartments across the narrow alleyway that stood so close you could stick an arm out the window and almost touch the bricks of the other building. The men took turn about at picking their favourite songs. Up next, Knox chose "Butterfly" by a one-hit-wonder band nobody remembered called Crazy Town. The tune technically contradicted the criteria they'd agreed on, having been released in the year 2000 and not being very grungy, but it was such a brilliant track that Sheehan agreed to allow it. They tapped pencils on the tabletop in time to the ethereal music. The tide on a bottle of Jack Daniels bourbon was about a third of the way out to sea when Knox's mobile rang.

'Jack?' said Knox, setting his iPhone to loudspeaker. 'Fire away.'

Lisbon half-heartedly apologised for the lateness of the call, then briefed the men on what had been learned after observing the CCTV video taken the day the mysterious McTaggart came to town.

'That's something to follow up, right?' Sheehan said before mixing a half nip of JD and cola in a teacup.

'Sure is,' agreed Knox. 'When I mentioned the murder of the ice-cream man, Elrod basically flew into a panic, couldn't get away quick enough. Elrod's involved, all right. But my hunch is it's on a very low level.'

'That's my feeling, too,' said Jack. 'He's not clever enough to organise his own life, let alone something as complicated as this.'

'So what's his role?' came the voice of Bruiser over the loudspeaker.

'From what the guv'nor described from the CCTV, I'd say Elrod Smart's met up with McTaggart outside the gym and passed on information regarding Jack's movements,' said Knox. 'Maybe he got paid for his trouble. Then the information got sent up the chain and the organiser set up the sting to snatch the kid.'

'How the fuck would Elrod know where I was going to be? I'm not exactly on Facebook posting selfies and being all *look at me, look at me* like so many mugs these days.'

'I'd say he found out via his sister,' said Knox. 'She in turn probably got it from your ex.'

'Not a chance!' exclaimed Jack. 'Sarah ain't gonna be telling all and sundry what I'm up to all hours of the day.'

'You sure?' Knox stopped to wipe up a puddle of drink.

They'd been taking it slowly with the booze, but with D-Day tomorrow, it was time to call it quits. 'Beauty salons are known to be hotbeds of gossip.'

'Damn!' said Jack. 'Let's grab this Elrod Smart prick and shake it out of him. Find out who he's reporting to. Where Skye is. What's his effin' address?'

Knox drained the last of his JD and coke. 'Me and Paddy shadowed him all night after he finished his shift. We lost him at one point, but I'd put a Hornet Micro tracker in his backpack and we soon picked up the scent again. There was maybe a 5-minute gap when we didn't have eyes on him. Any rate, his body language was all off the whole time. Jittery. Like a friggin' time-bomb ready to go off. Not sure I–'

'Cut to the chase, Micky. His address please.'

'Far be it from me to tell you how to do your job, guv, but I'm shit scared of what could happen if we make the wrong move now. If he suspects *we* suspect, he's likely to raise the alarm and put your daughter in immediate danger. More than she is already.'

'Not if we swoop now!'

'Here's another *what if*,' ventured Knox. 'Just say he's on the phone to whoever's running the show the very moment we try and grab him, hey? Game over. That's aside from the logistical issues.'

A heavy sigh from Jack. 'You're right, sunshine. I'm not being objective.'

'Understandable,' assured Sheehan. 'You're in a position none of us can begin to imagine.'

No one spoke for about ten seconds before Jack said, 'So, where do we go with the information we've got?'

This time the silent pause stretched for about thirty seconds.

'Not much we can do, unless you want to change your mind and make an official report to the police,' said Knox. 'It's not too late. Then they could hack Elrod's phone or whatever.'

Jack explained he'd promised Lars Pedersen he'd do exactly that if they failed to locate Skye by midday tomorrow.

'I think that's already today,' said Sheehan with a crackle in his voice.

'I bleedin' know that!' said Jack. 'Good night, lads. I'll be in touch in the morning. Hopefully with a workable plan, but I'm seriously running out of ideas.'

The phone disconnected on the other end and the two men exchanged blank looks. 'Shall we turn in?' said Sheehan.

Knox shook his head emphatically. 'No chance, you?'

'No. Too hyped up. I won't sleep until this thing is over. Your turn to pick a song.'

Sheehan chose one that a leading rock magazine had voted No. 24 on the all-time list of greatest ever grunge songs. 'This one's for Jack. A band from his new homeland.'

The pair closed their eyes and let the angst-ridden energy of Silverchair's classic "Tomorrow" wash over them.

The pair listened to over a hundred more songs and drank half a dozen instant coffees by sunrise. Eyes drooping, at 7:58am they were slurping frothy lattes and munching on take-away blueberry breakfast muffins from the café next door when Knox's iPhone rang. Jack. As per usual, Knox activated the loudspeaker.

'You fellas get any sleep?' said Lisbon.

'Nope. Me and Paddy were up all night. We're totally shagged out.'

'Pity,' said Jack without a trace of pity. 'Anyway, never mind.'

'What's up?'

'For you, Knox, a day and possibly an evening in front of your computer. But be prepared for anything.'

'And me?' said Sheehan eagerly.

'Wait at the front door. We're taking a long trip. Bruiser and I will pick you up.'

'When?'

A horn blared from the street below. 'Now. And bring a warm jacket.'

Chapter Twenty-One

One hour and thirty-five minutes earlier

HE CLIMBED out of the car, thanked Bruiser for driving him here and asked him to park a couple of blocks away and wait for further instruction. Bruiser gave a curt nod and sped off.

The watery yellow sun hadn't had time to chase the dew from the flowers when incognito Jack Lisbon approached the wrought iron gates of the park. White chem trails were already criss-crossing the brightening sky at 6:23am. Apparently a totally blue palette was a forlorn hope in western Europe's biggest city.

At the top of the three-metre arch two lions stood guard, a Latin motto underneath that Jack didn't understand, but it *should have* said, "All who enter beware". If only he'd been more observant yesterday. Such things were always easier in hindsight. On Sunday afternoon, like the lions, he'd been on guard, but not enough.

Logic now reared its head: snatching a child in broad

daylight could only have been achieved by professional criminals. In other words, none of the people on Bruiser's list could have organised it. They'd wasted precious time chasing shadows based on nothing but speculation.

Except for Elrod Smart. But they couldn't put pressure on him because, as Knox rightly pointed out, tipping off him – a person visibly agitated and unpredictable – presented enormous danger to Skye.

It was a Hail Mary play, but Jack had to check out the park one more time. Perhaps the police had missed clues when sweeping for evidence to assist the murder enquiry. He tugged the jaunty beret hard over the wig. A roomy beige trench coat loaned by Bruiser trailed down to the ankles. Not taking any chances, Jack effected a hobble and a stiff-armed gait to enhance the disguise.

A shiver ran down his spine as he retraced the steps he and Skye took yesterday. Along a winding path past the conservatory, a fenced-off play area, to the spot where he bought the ice-creams.

He located the bench from where Skye was abducted, sat on it and took a deep breath. *Think Lisbon, think.* He scrolled through the old Nokia N95, checked for updates on the murder enquiry – nothing made public yet about potential suspects, although police liaison did put out the usual call for witnesses. Whether anyone had come forward or not, the cops were keeping mum about it. Detectives had, though, officially ruled out robbery as a motive because the victim's leather money pouch was jammed full of notes and coins. Which was fuelling speculation by newspapers about a maniacal thrill killer getting their jollies by murdering people in broad daylight.

He couldn't help thinking about Jacob Buchbinder's unfortunate role in Jack's mess. Collateral damage in someone's evil plan to get at a one-time corrupt policeman. Wrong time for Jacob, wrong place. Although the police hadn't released important details about the investigation – such as the fact ice-creams were dumped beside the body and a child was abducted in the empty cart – Jacob's family were not holding back. His widow, Gisella, and their children were ripping into detectives for their weak response so far. They'd contacted every major news outlet in London, it seemed, and accused the Met of not taking the crime seriously. There was another case hogging the press lately, a high-profile politician at the scene of a sex scandal. Jacob's family slammed the police for devoting more energy to that than solving the brutal murder of their loving husband and father. Jack knew his deal with Pedersen was at least partly responsible for the bottleneck of information between police and the media. But for the moment, too bad.

He put the phone away and stood near the oak tree where the frisbee struck him, dropped to his hands and knees and searched the grass surrounding it. He looked between blades of grass, close enough to sniff the ground. He collected two cigarette butts and a red plastic button and placed them in a ziplock bag. Undoubtedly useless, but the process made him feel he was at least doing something. A further scrabble around on the lawn scored him a pound coin. Perhaps an omen of his luck changing. After examining an area of approximately ten square metres, he realised the scene contained nothing to help find his daughter.

The wind picked up and the temperature dropped a fraction as clouds began to gather. Soon, the heavens were much darker than when he arrived. A drop of rain, then another, soon – a shower. Despite the worsening conditions, people began to arrive on the common. Joggers and exercisers in sports gear, dedicated dog walkers, for whom rain was a mere inconvenience. Jack, too, was undeterred as he limped to the scene where that damned woman had sent him on a wild goose chase. Special punishment would be meted out to her. Nothing physical, Jack would never hit a woman, but he'd implore police prosecutors to throw the book at her.

Again, examination of the area where the woman had put on her act turned up no physical clues. Just expanses of lush, green grass, gravel paths and trees of every shape and size.

He headed back to where he bought the ice-creams. Exactly what Jack expected. Searching through the bushes where Jacob's body was found was another waste of time. The Met's Specialist Crime Command had thrown all its mighty resources into the forensics sweep. Crime tape flapping in the breeze, the scene had been cleared of all possible evidence.

He trod the path most likely taken by Jacob's killer with Skye inside the cart, eyes darting from one side to the other, then back to the middle of the path, hoping against hope some piece of evidence had been missed by the police. Again, a futile effort.

Finally, he reached the exit where the cart had been abandoned and, presumably, Skye had been transferred to a vehicle and whisked away, destination unknown. He strode a hundred metres in a westerly direction down the street, back to the starting point and then another hundred metres east. Then he crossed the street and traversed the same distance on the other side.

Again, nothing.

He reached into his pocket to make the call to Bruiser, but it was already buzzing.

Chapter Twenty-Two

07:45, Tuesday 13 March

'LARS.' Jack leaned his weary back against the oxidised green railing of the park's perimeter fence. His whole body ached, though he'd done no strenuous exercise since Sunday afternoon. Not sleeping had been a foolish idea. He was functioning on pure adrenaline now, in a state of semi-delirium. He'd eaten nothing for hours, his sense of balance was shot.

'Sorry for the early call but I've just checked my emails,' declared the Detective Chief Inspector. 'Good news.'

Jack turned and grabbed one of the thin metal poles for stability. Could this be it? 'You've found her?'

A cough. 'I said good news, not great news. We've tracked the IP attached to the link you sent me with the ransom demand.'

Not a hundred percent sure what this meant, Jack was nevertheless encouraged by the positive tone in Pedersen's voice. 'More details please, Lars. Don't leave me hanging, for God's sake.'

'OK. First of all, the link came with a "dot md" extension, which immediately needed investigating.'

'MD. What's that? Madagascar?'

'No. Moldova.'

Jack's heart thumped so hard he thought he'd drop dead on the spot. 'The kidnappers are in Moldova? That's part of the old Soviet Union. Crawling with Russian mafia. Holy shit, call Interpol. Call whoever you need to. I–' He dropped the hand holding the phone to his side. A kind of static noise rang in his head as he focused on a row of white Georgian terrace houses across the road. Then he heard the insistent voice.

'Please, Jack...can you hear me...Jack?'

He brought the phone back to his ear. 'Yes, I can hear you. I thought you said you had good news. This is a right fuckup. I'll never be able to live with myself. Jesus, once they realise the Bitcoins are no better than Monopoly money they'll kill her!'

'Stop raving for a minute, will you. It's taken a lot longer than I expected to finish the analysis because there was an extra level of encryption we had to uncloak to discover the IP. Yes, the URL *was* a Moldovan one, but that's irrelevant for our purposes. The IP address has been traced to the Orkney Islands. So whoever sent the ransom note most likely sent it from there, not Moldova.'

'Can you be sure of that?' Either the smog levels in London had instantaneously ramped up or Jack's lungs were about to pack it in. Either way, he could hardly breathe.

'My IT team tell me they've got no doubts. Moldovan extensions are becoming more common among cybercrooks, but often there's no real connection with the country. If the kidnappers had used a proxy server, then it would have been impossible. It seems kind of careless or arrogant they didn't do that. I'm leaning toward the latter.'

'Jesus, Lars. We both know arrogant criminals are the most dangerous kind.'

'I'm well aware of that.'

Jack's foot started tapping involuntarily. 'Can they pinpoint it to a physical address?'

A pause. 'Unfortunately, no. However they've narrowed it down to the island of Sanday.'

'Never heard of it.'

'I'd be surprised if you had. I've organised you a flight to the Orkney capital, Kirkwall. It leaves in two hours.'

'What?'

'I'll be accompanying you. On short notice, I've managed to scramble a task force together. When we arrive, officers from Police Scotland will take us to a secure location on the main island. From there we'll work out a plan to rescue Skye. It shouldn't be too difficult. There's only 550 people living on Sanday. This is something you could never have handled on your own.'

'Damn it, Lars. We had an agreement. I don't want the stormtroopers spooking a bunch of desperadoes holed up in…what was the name of that place again?'

'Sanday. Look, Jack. I'm sorry about this, but I'm rescinding that agreement. I've got a murder to solve and there's all kinds of pressure coming from above. Top brass want to know why we aren't going at the murder case like a steam train.'

'Bugger that. Surely the living take precedence over the dead. Especially when it's my daughter we're taking about.' An approaching jogger in a bright pink tracksuit looked askance at Jack as he ranted and waved his arms about. She must have though him deranged. Jack offered her a toothy smile which only made her run faster.

'I understand your reluctance, I really do, but be realistic. What are your options?'

'OK.' Pedersen was right, there were no other options left. 'I'll agree on one condition.'

'What's that?'

'I want two extra seats. For Lex Buskin and Patrick Sheehan.'

A sigh of frustration. 'That won't be easy, but I'll see what I can do. What are their dates of birth?'

'How the fuck would I know that? Text me what information you need for your protocols and I'll get back to you ASAP.'

A heavy sigh from Pedersen. 'Will do.'

Chapter Twenty-Three

09:47, Tuesday 13 March

THE UNMARKED BLACK BMW X5 delivered the three men and their high-ranking escort from Peckham to Battersea in a shade under fifteen minutes. Early morning commuter traffic was clogged with honking cars, crowded buses and swarms of furiously pedalling cyclists, but, as Bruiser quickly learned, real blues-and-twos work much better than Jack's horn-and-headlights version. Blue lights flashing and siren wailing, the skilled driver zipped in and out of tiny gaps and sped through intersections as his passengers held their breath.

The car squealed to a stop at the entrance to the ultra-modern facility on the banks of the river Thames. On a black circle emblazoned with a massive letter H at the end of a t-shaped jetty sat the sleekest helicopter Jack had seen in his life. The Leonardo AW109, a shiny red beast with silver trim, dwarfed two modest sight-seeing choppers stationed at the London Helipad. The earlier rain showers had cleared, the heavens delivering perfect weather for a vertical take off.

Three doors clunked as the men alighted. 'How the hell did you manage to organise this at short notice?' Jack shouted above the ambient din as Pedersen appeared by his side. 'I had to move heaven and Earth to get aviation support in Yorkville.'

DCI Pedersen touched the side of his nose. 'It's who you know, right?' He explained how he'd had to call in a favour from a contact in Aberdeen. Most National Police Air Service aircraft were already deployed around the country, and nothing available from the existing fleet could manage a non-stop trip to the Orkney Islands. 'The owner's an executive with an oil company. They usually charter massive Airbus Super Pumas to ferry workers back and forth from oil rigs in the North Sea. Those bad boys are way too big for this helipad to accommodate. This one's his private plaything, cost him over six million quid, so enjoy the ride.' Jack wondered what sort of "favour" warranted the loan of an expensive machine like this.

Pedersen turned his head, gestured for Bruiser and Sheehan to follow him and Jack to the waiting aircraft. 'All clearances have been approved by me. Let's roll.'

Jack gasped as he got closer to the helicopter, quickly zipped up his jacket as the turbulence caused by the spinning rotors threatened to rip the garment from his body. He ducked his head as an unsmiling man in a military green jumpsuit, black helmet and headphones held open the sliding door and waved the passengers inside.

This model was equipped to take seven persons: pilot and co-pilot, five in the main section in a three-opposite-two configuration. Jack and Pedersen sat in the twin seat, Sheehan and Bruiser either end of the triple seat, facing backwards as the chopper prepared to head for the far end of Scotland. The interior of the twin-engine Leonardo was plush, with soft leather seats and headrests, plenty of legroom and brushed chrome trims. Jack had anticipated something more rough-and-ready for this rescue mission. Instead, he felt like a celebrity VIP being whisked away to a luxury yacht off the coast of France.

The men buckled their harness seatbelts, donned Bose headsets, and within minutes the chopper elevated for a moment before tilting forward and whooshing off into the sky. Jack smiled thinly as Sheehan and Bruiser gawked out the windows through cupped hands and watched the landmarks grow smaller beneath them. On the drive to the helipad, Bruiser said he was an old hand at this caper, having taken several scenic flights over London. Sheehan confessed he had never been in a plane or a helicopter, but the lad showed no sign of nerves for a first-timer.

Once they had reached cruising altitude, the pilot read out the required safety instructions, information about the weather at their destination – temperature a chilly 7°C, heavily overcast with intermittent rain – and gave an ETA in Kirkwall of 11:55 if they maintained a speed of 300 kph. Pilot's spiel over, Pedersen removed his headset, touched Jack lightly on the knee and gestured for him to do the same. The top-of-the-line aircraft had superior sound insulation that negated the need to wear headsets unless you wanted to listen to music or communicate with the pilot and co-pilot. Sheehan and Bruiser continued to press their faces to the portholes.

'Lex Buskin I get,' said Pedersen, stretching his legs. 'He's a big, fit bloke. Brains to go with it. Why the kid, though?'

'He's motivated and he's got my back. Same as Lex.

And I know what they can do with their fists. I can't say the same for the goon squad that's going to assemble in Orkney to storm the beaches like it was effin' Normandy. Speaking of which, we don't even know where to start looking.'

'Yes we do.' Pedersen handed Jack a piece of paper. On it, a list of properties. Three general stores, farms and dozens of smaller holdings. Five of those were circled in blue marker pen.

'You reckon it has to be one of these?'

A slow nod. 'We've run a computer model that takes into account the infrastructure at these premises. Known residents. Occupations. Criminal records. A heap of other information from various sources.'

Jack ran his finger down the list. 'How do you suggest we narrow these five down to one?'

Pedersen took the paper and turned it over. Another four properties were circled on the reverse side.

'Shit, Lars, there's more? How do we figure out where they've got her without setting off alarm bells? It ain't exactly the Vietnamese jungle up there. I mean, it's all open expanse, innit? Nowhere to hide.'

Pedersen agreed it wouldn't be easy, and that's why the task force would be assembled in Kirkwall with a brief to determine the location and formulate a plan to swoop after sunset when the cover of darkness would assist in the open terrain. The gloomy weather would also be a bonus. No action would be taken without Jack's say-so. 'Officially, I also have to tell you that your ex-wife should know about what's happening. It's borderline criminal to keep the child's mother in the dark.'

'Unofficially?'

'Wait till it's over.'

'You're no fool, sunshine. She's a good mum but a loose

canon. A stray word from her probably got us in this mess in the first place. Any rate, I'll deal with any flack from her later.' He glanced at his watch. Thirty minutes gone, they'd be somewhere over Leicester or Nottingham by now, he guessed.

Sheehan had finally grown tired of staring out the window and was playing a game on his mobile. Bruiser's eyes were focused on a brochure describing the specs of the helicopter, head bobbing, Jack guessed to music he'd chosen from the vast entertainment menu. Jack had run out of energy to keep talking to Pedersen. His body demanded rest. He cracked his knuckles, kicked off his shoes, leaned back and fell into a dark, dreamless slumber.

Chapter Twenty-Four

12:05, Tuesday 13 March

KNOX LOGGED out of a complex stock trading spreadsheet to check his phone. A text message from Jack. They'd landed safely in Kirkwall, bang on schedule, now heading for a meeting with Scottish cops. Knox scratched his head, barely able to credit the weird turn of events over the last few days. He replied to the message. *Keep me in the loop. I double checked the crypto transaction settings, all A1 and ready to go.*

While he had the mobile out he decided to press the GPS app. Elrod Smart was on the move. Slowly walking down Copeland Road, which could mean he was heading to the lads' favourite pub from the old days. The blip stopped moving. The hornet confirmed Knox's suspicions.

Grab Jacket. Trot down stairs. Run to pub.

The Mare's Head was a classic London local, emerald green exterior, wood lined interior, rusted on regular drinkers. Years ago you'd be choking from the thick smoke, today the smell of stale beer seeped into the carpet was what greeted customers when they entered the establishment. Knox grabbed the brass handle and pushed open the heavy oak door. Inside, Sinead O'Conner's strong, clear soprano poured through the speakers, the smell of greasy food wafted from a backroom kitchen. Long-serving barman Eric the Red, so named on account of his shock of red hair and ginger Merlin's beard, looked up from polishing glasses and gave a friendly nod. Knox purchased a half pint of Abbott Ale and strolled past three generic, middle-aged punters perched at the far end of the bar nursing pints. According the micro tracker, accurate to 1.5 metres, Smart was located in another section of the pub. Knox glanced behind a partition wall. There he was, hunched on a stool, popping coins into a fruit machine, misery plastered all over his face.

'Oi!' said Knox. 'Fancy meeting you here.'

'Yeah, fancy.' Another coin clattered into the belly of the machine.

Knox pulled up a stool and pumped a couple of pound coins into a neighbouring metallic box. 'Thought any more about our proposition?'

'I already agreed to it.' He turned, shot Knox a suspicious glare. 'What's your game then? I ain't seen you in this pub for a long time. What's going on?'

An awkward laugh. 'I missed the joint. Can't a man visit his favourite local without being interrogated? Sheesh.' Knox pressed some random buttons, fluked a small win. 'Wow, check this, Smarty. Three quid on that spin.'

'Whatever.' His tone said *look at that prick rubbing it in.* 'Anyhow, why are you here?'

'I won't lie.' *Yes I will.* 'I wanted to make sure you were happy with the money we're offering you for the training sessions.'

'Since you mention it, no, not really. I mean, you say it's gonna be almost no-holds-barred stuff, yeah?'

A nod of affirmation.

'Well, I ain't got no proper health insurance, know what I mean? If I get hurt and I can't work, I don't get paid. So I need a bit more to compensate.'

Knox stroked his chin. The man had a point. *If* such a scheme were to go ahead. Which it wouldn't. 'How about double?'

'Triple.'

'Sure.'

'Let me know when you're ready to start.' Smart pulled out his phone, scrolled for a moment, put it back in his pocket. 'I gotta go back to work.'

Knox noticed the lack of a uniform, said nothing except good-bye. He'd keep tracking him, shadowing from a distance. He downed the rest of his beer, headed for the exit. Before he could escape, Eric waved Knox over. 'You used to be one of my best customers. Three or four Abbotts every Friday night, up to six on a Saturday if I recall. Where've you been hiding?'

'Nowhere.' Knox patted his stomach. 'You might notice this is flatter than a day-old Guinness.'

'Aye, so it is.' The man grinned as he wiped the wooden bar top. 'Upped the training have ya?'

'Nope. I just don't feel the need for so much alcohol these days. I've got a business to run.'

The men exchanged a few more pleasantries before Knox thought to press the barman about Smart. Had he noticed anything odd about him lately?

'That lad's always been up and down like a yo-yo, so to me his behaviour's what I'd call normal.'

'Did you hear about the ice-cream man murdered on the common?'

'Aye, terrible. What's the world coming to?'

'Any of the punters have any theories?'

Eric chuckled. 'Sure. And they're all different.' He leaned forward, dropped his tone a fraction. 'But I will tell you something weird.'

'What's that?'

'There was this big Scottish fella in the other night. Glasgow accent. I could almost tell ye the neighbourhood he's from.'

'Was his name McTaggart?'

'I don't know, but he approached a few of the regulars and asked them about Jack Lisbon.'

'Is that right?'

'Yeah. But get this. Just before he left he made a phone call, standing right in front of me he was. He said to the person on the other end of the line: *No one knows anything Mr McNair.* Now, I'm not sure, but isn't the name of that boxing gym up the street McNair's?'

Back outside Knox walked 50 metres up the road, huddled under an alcove outside a greengrocer's. He dialled Jack's burner phone. No answer. He left a short message.

Fifteen minutes later, back at his flat, he trawled the Internet for information on anyone called McNair on the Orkney Island of Sanday. Only one search return – a snippet from a decade-old newspaper article about a fundraiser for the renovation of the Sanday Community Hall. It contained a photo of a smiling man of average height, average build and, from what Knox could make out under the big, woolly hat pulled low over his eyes, average appearance. The caption read. *Visitor to our fair island, Donald McNair, holidaying at Brigalow Farm with his wife Muriel, donates £100 to the cause.*

He called Jack again. No answer, second message left.

The Micro Hornet tracker app showed Smart wasn't at work, but had gone home. Knox returned his attention to his drop-shipping accounts, which were motoring alone nicely, but left on the hornet tracker app's map within view. Just in case Smart got itchy feet.

Chapter Twenty-Five

12:37, Tuesday 13 March

DETECTIVE SUPERINTENDENT JULIAN CALTHORPE from Police Scotland pinned tiny red flags on a detailed topographic map of the island of Sanday. The shape of the long, thin 20 square mile island reminded Jack of a seahorse. He counted the flags – nine, to match the list of properties Pedersen and his officers had compiled. Evenly spread out, on coastal and inland locations. Bruiser and Sheehan stood on the opposite side of the table, eyes agog.

'You see here,' Calthorpe pointed at a green flag. 'That's where the rigid inflatable Zodiac boat will land as soon as it starts getting dark, around 19:20. It's not completely dark until 20:26, so there will be some chance of being observed, which is not ideal. However, camouflage and stealth will be our strengths here. We could wait until zero visibility to mount the operation, but the deadline the kidnappers set makes that too risky in terms of the child's welfare. Six ARV officers, detectives Lisbon and Pedersen will–'

'What about us?' interrupted Sheehan, bouncing on his toes.

'I'll get to that,' Calthorpe replied sharply. 'Each member of the team will wear a set of Fenn night-vision goggles, and be armed with Glock 17 pistols. In addition two officers will be carrying H&K assault rifles.'

'Holy shit.' Sheehan again. 'I've never held a gun in my life.'

'Me either,' added Bruiser.

'That's not a problem,' said Calthorpe.

'It's not?' said Sheehan.

'No, because you two shall remain right here.'

'Come on,' said Jack. 'They've come all this way to stay inside when I need them most? You must be joking!'

'With all due respect, Detective Lisbon, it's not your decision to make. I'm already sticking my neck out allowing you to go along, considering you no longer have authority to enforce the law on British soil.'

'But...'

'No buts. I'm sure you have confidence in your... colleagues here. However I cannot allow them to take part in an exfiltration operation of this nature. They don't have the proper training. The very idea is, again with all due respect, completely ludicrous. Team members for this operation are you, DCI Pedersen and six of our ARV officers. End of story.'

Jack ran his hand across his face, sweat starting to leak through the pores at the back of his neck and in his armpits despite the coldness of the room. He counted to ten in his head, fighting the urge to plant a fist in the moustachioed commander's face. By the time he reached ten, he had to admit, Calthorpe was absolutely right. Why had Jack even insisted these men come along? Then he realised, it was for moral support. And to have them close by even for that, he was grateful the decision-makers had acquiesced.

'OK, sir.' Addressing the man in charge with respect also somehow seemed fitting now.

'That's better,' said Calthorpe flatly. 'But don't despair, your friends can assist us by keeping things tidy here at the command post, and running errands to the shops in town should we need supplies.'

Jack had expected crestfallen frowns on the faces of Sheehan and Bruiser. But no, what he detected from their suddenly loose shoulders was a sense of relief. The idea of heroic injury or death may have been appealing in the abstract, not in reality.

He turned his attention back to the broad-shouldered Scots commander. Out of the corner of his eye, Jack caught an exchange of knowing looks between him and Pedersen. *Sneaky pair of bastards, stitching me up.* Back to business, he asked: 'Sir, I'm wondering, how are we going to get from the landing point to any of these nine buildings. Walk? The distances are too great.'

Pedersen nodded. 'Good point.'

Calthorpe fondled his bushy moustache as he leaned forward. A pair of loose-fitting spectacles threatened to slide down his nose and onto the table before he stopped them with a forefinger. 'One of our officers delivered a van to Sanday by ferry this morning and returned as a foot passenger just a few minutes ago. The van is large enough to transport the entire squad plus equipment, including weapons and state-of-the-art laser microphones to pinpoint the location of persons inside the premises. You will find the van here, 100 metres or so from where the Zodiacs will beach at the shore of the Bay of Stove. Team members will transfer to this van, and Constable Jessop over there' –

Shot to the Heart

Calthorpe pointed to a lean man leafing through a ring binder thick with papers – 'will drive you all to the destination where the exfiltration will take place.'

'Oh, and that destination would be which of these flags?' said Jack, trying in vain to keep the sarcasm out of his voice. There were too many guessing games going on, with Skye's fate in the balance.

'The time is now...' Calthorpe turned robotically to a clock on the wall behind him...'12:47. You've indicated the kidnappers will contact you after the cryptocurrency transaction is made at 8:00pm to give you further instructions. That gives us a lot of time to keep investigating. I'm confident the team will crack it in time.'

'And if they don't?'

'Then we wait and see what message you receive. I'm sure once they've revealed their hand, our decision will be made for us.'

Jack declined responding to that. He knew the answer. Ram down the doors of each of the nine flagged buildings, and if Skye wasn't in any of them, raid every home and interrogate every citizen on the island until they found her. And if they still couldn't find her...that was not worth thinking about.

'Try and take heart, Detective Lisbon. The operation is in very capable hands.' Calthorpe gestured towards the six officers in civvies sitting at small tables dotted about the room. The ad hoc team under Calthorpe's command had requisitioned a two-storey yellow-and-red sandstone cottage less than 200 metres from the historic St Magnus Cathedral in Kirkwall. Most of them had their eyes riveted on a glowing laptop screen. They were elite, ex-military and intelligence personnel now retrained as Police Scotland Armed Response Vehicle, or ARV officers, capable of thinking and acting under immense pressure. Now and then Jack scanned their faces – concentration etched on each one. Occasionally they'd stop to stretch or take a sip of water, slip out to an enclosed back courtyard for a sly smoke. Their task – to analyse every piece of information they could find about the island of Sanday that could help pinpoint Skye's location and, by extension, the location of whoever killed Jacob Buchbinder on the common.

Even as the cops' purposeful activity inspired confidence, Jack's heart began to weigh heavy with dread. It dawned on him that, unless the kidnappers had spies tracking his every move, they'd be assuming Jack was still in London, waiting to learn from them what his next move would be. In particular, where to go to pick up his daughter. But surely they didn't expect him to hightail it all the way to the Orkney Islands for the handover. So…were they intending to hand her over at all? Was she even alive? *Was she even here?* Shit, the more he thought about it, the worse the scenarios.

He looked at Bruiser and Sheehan, staring at their feet. He toyed with the idea of apologising for dragging them along for no reason, but a smart-thinking ARV officer spared Jack the bother. The man handed Bruiser a shopping list of supplies and a fold-up tourist map. Jack heard the words: *no need to rush back.* The Londoners headed out the side door with half-smiles on their faces. There was no need to apologise, it was still an adventure to them.

DCI Pedersen stood from behind a desk, took Jack by the crook of the arm and led him to a small table topped with a tea urn and plates of fruit and energy snacks. 'I just got a report back from my IT team.' He grabbed a banana and started peeling it. 'We finally got a match on the CCTV.'

'What? I thought…'

'Not the face, but the tattoo on his right shoulder.'

'Of course. There are separate databases for inkwork. We had a case in Yorkville a couple of years ago where a tattoo proved critical in the arrest of a serial killer.'

Pedersen nodded. 'Twenty percent of the adult population in the UK have at least one tattoo, can you believe it? In 25 to 40-year-olds it's thirty percent.'

'Yeah, yeah, fascinating. What did you learn about McTaggart?' Jack dropped a teabag into a Styrofoam cup, poured boiling water and added a splash of milk, stirred in two sugars. Then he realised how exhausted he still was, added another sugar. Pedersen was content to drink mineral water.

'His name isn't McTaggart, it's Alistair Gordon. He served in the Highlanders, 4th Battalion, did a tour of Afghanistan. All his details are on record.'

'Where is he now?'

'My guess – on Sanday. Where he's been and what he's been up to since his discharge from the army is anyone's guess. Relatives and a host of old army buddies have been contacted, they know nothing, or at least claim to know nothing. He's somehow managed to keep his nose very clean indeed. To the point of invisibility.'

'He's going to need every bit of that military training when I get hold of the bastard,' said Jack through gritted teeth.

'Keep speaking like that and you can keep your pals company when we strike tonight. For now, I'll pretend I didn't hear those words.'

The non-threatening tone of Pedersen's voice left no doubt the DCI would look the other way if Jack decided to mete out his own brand of justice.

The two men retreated to a couch with their tea. Pedersen made a call to his office, ostensibly to ask if there had been any developments in the Jacob Buchbinder case. Frustration and exhaustion were proving a bad combination for Jack. Even resting quietly, he sensed his pulse rate and blood pressure were at levels his doctor would be concerned about. With nothing better to do to pass the time but wait, he pulled out his phone. There were some old-school games installed on the clunky Nokia, maybe one of them would calm his nerves. No time for that – there were two missed messages from Knox, only minutes between them.

Jack listened to the messages, felt his heart rate shift up another gear. This was the news he'd been waiting to hear.

With Pedersen still nattering on his mobile, Jack dashed to where Calthorpe was studiously eyeing the flags on the map. 'Sir.'

'Yes, Detective Lisbon?'

Jack quickly explained that Knox had found a link between Alistair Gordon aka McTaggart and a Mr McNair.

'Who the hell is McNair?' Calthorpe stroked his cheek. 'Pretty sure that name hasn't come up anywhere.'

Jack could feel his body trembling. 'No, sir. Sometimes all the best technology in the world can't beat good-old face-to-face questioning. And a bit of luck.'

'Stop rambling, man.'

'I saw the name Stanhope was on your list. Check that out. Something in the recesses of my mind's telling me that's important, too.'

'Whoa, back it up. You haven't finished telling me about McNair yet.'

'It's the name of the gym in Peckham I used to train at.'

'And?' Calthorpe's lush eyebrows arched.

'Donald McNair is the son of the man who started the

gym back in the 1960s, Angus McNair. My man on the ground found an old newspaper clipping of McNair junior holidaying on Sanday ten years ago.'

'Right. That's too much of a coincidence.' He grabbed Jack on the shoulder and gave it a firm squeeze. 'Well done.'

Calthorpe gave a loud handclap, silencing the humming HQ. All personnel removed headsets and looked up like inquisitive puppies. He imparted what Jack had just told him. 'I want everyone on the same job. First one to crack it gets an extra three days off on top of their next holidays. Cross-check the name Donald McNair with every property on Sanday, not just the flagged ones. Go!'

Within five minutes, Detective Constable Fiona O'Toole shot her hand up in the air and called out "Bingo!" She stood and read her findings, in one of those delicate Scottish accents characteristic of people who have spent many years living in England.

'Brigalow Farm, *not* one of the flagged properties' – a slight gasp arose from the officers assembled – 'is owned by a woman called Carmen Stanhope. She inherited the house from her deceased mother. Carmen resides in Edinburgh, rents out her farmhouse as a holiday let in summer. The rest of the year the place stands idle. Her father is Donald McNair, resident of East Kilbride, South Lanarkshire. A handful of minor criminal charges, all drugs related, no custodial sentences. Interestingly, he was questioned in relation to his wife's suspicious death by drowning seven years ago but no charges were laid against him.'

Jack scratched his head. Why would the son of the noble boxer Angus McNair want to kidnap *my* daughter? The very idea was preposterous. If McNair junior had been following the investigation into the murder of Alex Gallagher and had, like many others, suspicions Jack did it, surely the man would be grateful, not filled with ideas of vengeance. It didn't make sense. Right now the whys and wherefores mattered little. He just wanted Skye back.

'Right,' said Calthorpe. He gathered everyone around the map, removed all the red flags and placed one of them back on Brigalow farm. 'We need to find out if there's anyone staying at the farmhouse. If there is, that's our target confirmed. We may need to have another look at satellite imagery, see if there have been any lights on at the property over the last few days.'

'No need for that, sir.' A stocky officer with spikey blonde hair tapped a fingernail next to the flag. 'I happened to drive past that place when I delivered the van this morning. There are people there, all right. I saw two vehicles – a mud-splattered tradesman's van and a black SUV. I checked the motor vehicle registry while DC O'Toole was speaking just now and, surprise, surprise. A Donald Neil McNair of East Kilbride owns a black Kia Sportage.'

The room let out a whoop, to the very last officer. Rescuing a child from harm – there was no more important job. The real hard work, Jack knew, was still ahead of them.

Chapter Twenty-Six

14:11, Tuesday 13 March

DONALD MCNAIR BENT LOW, stoked the open fire with a metal poker, trying to generate more heat in this godforsaken hovel. Embers glowed at the bottom of the ash pile, set a small log aflame. He took a deep breath and exhaled, watched the cloud of condensation gather before his face then disappear. The supply of wood from the barn was running out, but that was OK. They'd be leaving the island on the ferry tomorrow at 10:45. Then he'd drive the Kia from Kirkwall back to East Kilbride, while Brinkworth and Gordon drove the kid to London, dropped her off in a back alley in the Dog Kennel Hill Estate, and contact Lisbon with the pickup address. Operation complete.

He went to the small study at the side of the kitchen, sat back behind his desk. He inspected the custom-made webserver; lots of green lights flashing meant all the equipment was working fine. Then a quick surf of the Internet for any news of Skye Lisbon. Nothing. Perfect. Her father had kept his word and not raised the alarm. Which meant he would surely make the payment. If not, the kid wouldn't be making the trip back to London. There was plenty of soft ground on the farm; Gordon and Brinkworth could dig a great big hole and drop her in it. She'd never be found.

Another ear-splitting scream rent the cool air inside Brigalow farmhouse. Where did the kid get the energy? They'd only fed her two slices of bread and some dry crackers since she was delivered to the house. During the war the Germans kept their prisoners passive by maintaining them on a starvation diet, and that seemed like a good idea to McNair. Unfortunately, it didn't seem to be working too well on this girl. Perhaps she'd inherited some of her father's spirit.

'Alistair, go up and see what that brat wants, will ye?'

'You should have made Suzie come with us. We need her here. She woulda been better at handling the kid.'

'Yeah, well, she had better things to do, like restock my liquor cabinet at home. So I'm appointing you nanny for now. I pay you enough, don't I?'

'Sometimes I wonder about that.' Ex-soldier Alistair Gordon leaned back in his chair, arms folded across his beefy chest.

'Well, after 8:00pm you'll be wondering no longer.'

'You sure he's going to pay up?'

'Wee Elrod tells me Lisbon's besotted with the lassie, so, yeah, I'm sure. He knows the consequences if he fails to comply.'

Another scream from upstairs, louder then ever.

'Are you still here, Alistair? Wait, hang on.' McNair shuffled to a battered old fridge, pulled out a bowl of baked beans, crusty around the edges. 'See if you can bribe her into shutting up with this. If she plays up, put the gag back on her.'

'Aye.' Gordon took the bowl, grabbed a grotty spoon from a drawer and trod up the stairs. McNair heard him yell at her to shut up or she'd be getting no dinner.

McNair gave silent thanks for Gordon. A loyal foot soldier, there was nothing the man wouldn't do for his boss. McNair hated kids, and kidnapping one for ransom rankled his conscience not one iota.

His own precious Carmen was an exception. A tough kid to raise, she stood by her father when the case went to court. She couldn't entertain the idea her dad would intentionally hurt his wife, *her beloved mother*. And she said as much to the police. Perhaps that swung the matter, perhaps it was the lack of physical evidence. He had made sure Maureen's seatbelt would stay jammed – he'd broken the mechanism weeks before, so that the thing getting stuck was nothing new. He made a point of complaining about it to a mechanic friend who later testified he knew about the dodgy buckle, but never got around to checking it. McNair had the foresight to book a car service to be carried out two days *after* he planned to drive the vehicle into the dam, with a special instruction to fix the damned seatbelt. Carmen knew the buckle was suss, too. When she got to ride in the front seat with dad, he made a fuss about helping her get it undone every time. So, it just had to have been an accident. And he'd gotten away with it. But the financial payoff was so lousy he may as well not have even gone to the effort. It turned out Maureen had recently changed her will, leaving everything to Carmen, including her life-insurance and the ruinous ancestral farmhouse on Sanday. As much as Carmen loved her dad, she'd inherited his greed and wouldn't part with a penny of the insurance money, plus she was adamant she'd never sell the property to him. It served as a memorial to mum. However, he could use it during the off season if he wanted to go for a "getaway". On the bright side, the dive into the dam did serve a long-term purpose in securing his freedom. Maureen had, over the years, turned from doting wife into an unbearable nagging cow, always raving on about his drinking and drug taking and...

'Oi, did you hear me?' said Gordon, shaking McNair by the shoulder.

'What?' McNair noticed baked beans and tomato sauce stuck to the man's shirt.

'I had to put the gag back on. And another set of cable ties. I had a hard job of it pinning her down. Next time you can give me a hand.'

'Bugger off. Brinkworth can help you. By the way, where is he?'

'Said he was going fishing.'

'Fuck's sake, man! I told you we have to keep our heads down.'

'Come on, Donny. The neighbours have seen all of us out in the yard, fetching wood and what not. They know we're here. Sitting inside all the time's gonna look even more suspicious than taking a wee walk now and again, don't you think?'

McNair had to admit the logic of that, but still...He felt like a sitting duck here on this windswept island at the gates of hell. He told Gordon to leave him in peace for a while, he needed time to himself.

McNair made himself a strong Yorkshire tea with two teabags, lit a cigarette and dialled his man in London.

'Yes?' The voice lacked all vitality. McNair couldn't wait

for the project to come to its successful conclusion, if only to be rid of this pathetic sad sack.

'What's the news on Lisbon?'

'Ah...I haven't been able to keep tabs on him like you wanted.'

McNair stood, tipped his seat over until it crashed against the wall. Giving the lad a bollocking would be fun just for the sake of it. 'What the hell do you mean? I offered you another hundred quid to stay the course!'

'There's a problem.'

'What kind of a problem?' Surely there was nothing to worry about. Lisbon was the one who ought to be worrying, not McNair.

'He's skipped town.'

'What d'ye mean, skipped town?'

'I know this is going to sound ridiculous, but Phoebe told me Lisbon took the kid to Cornwall.'

'Come again?'

'He told his ex he took the girl on a fast train to Cornwall for a seaside holiday.'

Smart was half correct, McNair mused. Only it was a completely different seaside the lassie was at, a freezing shite one where you couldn't enter the water without getting hypothermia. 'Thanks for the information. The cheque's in the mail.' McNair ended the call. There would be no more money, the kid had outlived his usefulness. Any sign of a leak from him to Lisbon or the law and Gordon would tear him to pieces. When Brinkworth returned from his walk, with a bonus bucket of sea trout, McNair gathered the men together for a celebratory whisky.

'Lisbon's so rattled, he's had to invent a story for his ex wife. In other words, he's shitting his pants. Which means the Bitcoins are as good as in the bank. Cheers!'

The three men raised shot glasses and despatched the smooth 16-year-old single malt. Yes, McNair thought to himself, it was all going nicely. He'd even cook some chips and fry up a bit of fish for the poor wee lassie upstairs. As long as Lisbon didn't decide to play games, it wouldn't be the last meal she ever ate.

Chapter Twenty-Seven

17:49, Tuesday 13 March

JACK TUGGED the lightweight all-terrain boots over a thick pair of socks, tied the laces in a tight double bow. Tripping over them at a crucial moment could cost someone's life. The last piece of the uniform puzzle in place, he sat back up straight so ARV officer Constable Craig Jessop, designated driver and makeup artist, could apply a layer of camo face paint. DCI Pedersen sat beside Jack, waiting his turn for a makeover. Both men were dressed the same as their counterparts –thermal undershirts, black pants and Gore-Tex 2-layer jackets. The only missing items were the black ballistic helmets that would be carried in hand until it was time to don them onboard the Zodiac. All personnel would be issued Glock 17s; in addition, two of the ARV officers would be toting Heckler & Koch G36 assault rifles. Jack had no idea of the weaponry or resources of the kidnappers or even how many of them there were; he prayed the manpower and arsenal assembled here in Kirkwall would be enough.

Fully kitted out, the team assembled in an alley behind the ad hoc headquarters for a final brief from DSU Calthorpe. The atmosphere was at once sombre and optimistic. Calthorpe announced he'd be staying behind with an extra officer just arrived from Aberdeen to coordinate, plus Bruiser and Sheehan, returned from their sightseeing tour of the capital. Bruiser, bless him, bought Jack a couple of packets of spearmint gum.

A horn tooted at the end of the alley. The team boarded a rumbling blue farmer's lorry that whisked them to the nearby Kirkwall West Pier where a Severn class lifeboat awaited them. On the way, DC Brodie Chesterfield, in situ commander of the operation, took the opportunity to read out some facts about the vessel from a sheet of notes. Nearly 60 feet long, 42 tons and a top speed of 25 knots. Jack, totally unimpressed by those stats, preferred to observe the unhurried life of locals going about their business along Harbour Street. Within minutes the lorry made a left turn onto the long, broad concrete pier. Among an assortment of fishing boats, tugs and ferries, the chunky black-and-orange lifeboat stood out like a beacon. Behind her bobbed the Zodiac Hurricane ZH-940 OB that would transport them to the island of Sanday. The lifeboat itself could handle virtually any weather, which was good news as conditions were starting to cut up rough – whistling winds and choppy small waves even in the shelter of the harbour, with a forecast of possible gale-force winds towards midnight. Looking at the boat jiggling about on its moorings, Jack wondered if he should have mentioned his predisposition to sea-sickness. Not necessary, he figured, because a wildly rocking boat could never make him sicker than the thought of Skye coming to harm.

Boarding the boat via a rattling aluminium gangway, Jack tucked in behind DC Fiona O'Toole, apparently the best pistol shooter amongst them and as fit and strong as her male teammates. Nearly as broad in the shoulders as Jack and only half an inch shorter, she strode the plank with the confidence of a Viking woman. He followed the heels of her boots all the way inside the vessel.

Already onboard in the wheelhouse were the helmsman, coxswain, navigator and engineer. The helmsman, sporting a nautical white beard, appeared in the medical section where the officers were waiting, and quickly ushered them to the top of a short flight of stairs leading to the so-called survivor area, with seating for twelve. 'We'd better get cracking,' he said. 'The sooner we get you transferred to the Zodiac, the sooner we can make ourselves available for at-sea rescues.' The man huffed and puffed under his breath as he gestured for the team to head down the stairwell, as if rescuing a little girl on land was less important than saving people "at sea". Jack jutted out his chin and sneered at the supercilious git, who took a step backwards before retreating into the wheelhouse.

Once strapped into his seat, which was not unlike those in the helicopter that brought him to the island, the reality of the situation struck home. The old cliché held true — failure was not an option.

The helmsman wasn't exaggerating his eagerness to depart. No sooner were the officers seated than the boat's twin engines engaged. The vessel began to chug out of the harbour at a steady clip. Out of the confines of the harbour, it headed northwards. The route was simple: skirt the west coast of the island of Shapinsay, thence continue northeast to the bottom tip of the island of Eday, where the transfer to the RIB would take place.

After 45 minutes of ploughing through the rough sea, an announcement came over the loudspeaker. *We've arrived at the transfer point, the Bay of Backaland.* And not a moment too soon either, thought Jack. He'd been battling the entire journey to keep his breakfast in his stomach and off the rubber matting under his boots. Fuel and oil fumes and other machine odours emanating from the engine room hadn't helped matters; only by concentrating fully on the job ahead had he subdued the urge to puke.

DC Chesterfield quickly took command, rose to his full 6'4", and instructed the team to fall into line behind him and make their way into the Zodiac. On the top deck the officers had to spread their legs for balance, and then lean into the buffeting wind and lower their heads as they inched their way forward.

First onto the rubber craft were Chesterfield and Jessop. Next, Detective Constables John Harper, Trevor Islington and Moheer Khan, each carrying bags of equipment to be doled out before the raid, and Fiona O'Toole. Jack was second-last to descend the ladder into the boat, DCI Pedersen, strangely quiet the entire journey – perhaps he also had a propensity for *mal de mer* – was last. Jack felt his foot slip slightly upon touching the surface of the horseshoe-shaped inflated rubber tube that kept the boat afloat. His heart skipped a beat and he caught his breath. DC O'Toole must have seen him wobble, grabbed his hand and escorted him to a seat in the middle of the craft. Smart woman – the closer to the centre of a boat, even landlubber Jack knew, the lesser the disorienting effects of pitching and rolling on the human organism. Jack closed his eyes, let the sea spray wash over his face.

Commander DC Chesterfield turned, made sure all members were seated. He grabbed the wheel with one hand and pulled the throttle with the other, the bow of the high-powered boat rose steeply and they thundered towards the shores of the island of Sanday. Cold salty spray covered everyone as the boat bounced from wave to juddering wave. The impact of some landings was so hard Jack thought his pelvis was going to crack.

With the landing point heaving into view through a soup of rain and salt spray, Jack patted a pocket on his left breast. His regular mobile phone with the London SIM card inside. The one McNair would contact Jack on with instructions. So far since the initial message, the bastard had been quiet. Whether that was a good or bad sign, only time would tell.

A subconscious check of his watch. 18:39. One hour and twenty-one minutes until McNair's deadline. His hand felt the comforting bulk of the Glock under his jacket. He hadn't fired a gun in the field for two years. Today, he'd happily empty the contents of the magazine into the head of every bastard who had a hand in abducting his daughter.

Chapter Twenty-Eight

18:52, Tuesday 13 March

THE ZODIAC GLIDED to a stop on a narrow crescent of dirty-white sand. Grass, thorny weeds and low stone walls presented the only screen between the officers and nearby outbuildings. Loose bricks lay in a jumble around what appeared to be barns either awaiting repair or crumbling to the ground and abandoned. There were two other ramshackle dwellings within a 100 metre radius of the landing point, however DC Jessop had already confirmed they were unoccupied. Around 350 metres distant, giant windmills spun hard in the gusty conditions. One thing Jack noticed was missing from the island – the natural cover provided by trees.

All officers heaved and dragged the Zodiac towards a pile of lichen-encrusted boulders, tucked the craft behind them. Jessop drove the claw anchor deep into the sand. Chesterfield pointed to a matte black van that stood like a silhouette by one of the old barns. The vehicle would take them as close as possible to Brigalow farm while remaining out of view of the house. From there it would be commando-style crawling once it was deemed dark enough to proceed. Chesterfield led the team to the waiting van. He fished out a set of keys, unlocked the vehicle with a blip, opened the back doors and clambered inside followed by the others, bar Jessop and O'Toole, who sat in the front cabin: he the driver, she – the lookout.

The officers arranged themselves along built-in benches inside the extra-long wheel base Ford Transit 350L. A tangle of khaki webbing hung from the walls, giving the impression they were heading into a war zone. DC Khan unzipped a duffel bag and handed around tactical waterproof comms headsets, which were quickly checked for operability, and extra clips for the Glock pistols. All officers could hear each other well through the cans, which had a range of 600 feet, more than enough for this operation. Islington divvied up the night goggles and rubber-handled knives in leather sheaths which the officers clipped to their utility belts. Harper took an assault rifle for himself and handed the other to Pederson. Jack raised an eyebrow, having figured the weapon was destined for one of the ARV officers. Pedersen inspected the H&K like he used one every day, which, for all Jack knew, he did.

'OK, listen up. Let's go over the plan one more time.' Chesterfield spoke in a well-modulated, assured voice. The plummy accent hinted at an expensive private education. 'We will drive for about 3 kms before we reach the last bend in the road leading to the farm. A hedge and a derelict outbuilding will keep us out of the direct line of sight of the farm. Please refer to the printed maps showing the plan of the house and surrounds.' Chesterfield gave the officers a minute to once again study the maps. He continued, 'There are eight of us, split into four pairs – me and DS Lisbon, O'Toole with Pedersen, Harper with Islington, Jessop with Khan, each taking one side of the house. Each pair will aim laser microphones, which DC Khan will distribute just before we disembark the van, at windows. For the benefit of Detectives Pedersen and Lisbon – the microphones are sensitive enough to pick up any conversation in the house, so lack of visuals won't be a big problem.' His lips curved into the trace of a smile.

'It's still a *bit* of a problem, though, isn't it?' said Islington. 'I mean, they could be sitting by the fire quietly reading copies of "The People's Friend" or doing bleedin' crossword puzzles.'

Chesterfield nodded understandingly. 'Good point. However, we're getting closer and closer to the deadline set by the kidnappers. I think it's fair to assume there'll be quite a bit of chatter going on. They'll be excited, thinking they're about to win a fortune in ransom.'

Jack snorted under his breath. Like hell they'll win anything, damn them to hell!

The commander's explanation made perfect sense to the troops, who kept their heads turned towards him. His eyes expanded as if he'd suddenly remembered something important. He held up his hand and asked the team to be quiet while he called Calthorpe on his mobile phone, loudspeaker engaged.

'Got any intel results for us re security, sir?'

Before departing HQ the officers had discussed a disconcerting question: what if there are dogs on the property or a motion sensor alarm system? Calthorpe and the officer fresh from Aberdeen, DC Vince Dutra, had undertaken to find out. 'No dogs, according to the neighbour we managed to contact,' said Calthorpe. 'With a caveat: *as far as she's aware.* The woman has a sensitive terrier of her own and she said it would bark like crazy if it sensed another dog was there. She walks her dog past Brigalow farmhouse every morning and so far it's not reacted at all. She can confirm she's seen three different men about the place, friendly enough, but she reckons they give her the willies.'

'Thank you sir. What about evidence of security installations?'

'No local electricians or security firms in the Orkney Islands that we've been able to contact have admitted to setting up anything at the farmhouse, although there's no guarantee the kidnappers haven't done it themselves. My instinct tells me it's unlikely they've taken precautions. People like them are arrogant in their belief that they're too clever for the law. That said, I advise you to tread very carefully.'

'Roger that, sir. We do have an electronic alarm jammer in our arsenal that I'll activate once we're in range, just in case. I'll be in touch when we're done.'

'OK. Good luck to all of you. You've got a wee girl to bring home.' Calthorpe disconnected the call.

Chesterfield returned his attention to the team. 'OK, where was I? Right. Last word on our kit. One of each pair of officers will be carrying a couple of G60 stun grenades. Use these if you feel it can give you an advantage without having to fire weapons. DC Khan, can you please distribute these.'

Khan handed out the devices as requested to the commander, Jessop and Islington. Jack had overheard some officers on the lifeboat talking about "flashbangs". He guessed that meant these stun grenades.

Chesterfield then gave a timeline for moving in, depending on the results of the audio surveillance or if the target showed their hand in some other way. He gave Jessop the signal to drive on. Jack figured the roads must be in fair condition – just a couple of jolts from potholes compared to the washing-machine treatment out on the ocean. He sensed the vehicle take a slight left-hand bend, then come to a gentle stop.

'We getting out now?' said Jack to no one in particular.

'Not yet,' replied Chesterfield. 'Sit tight, I'll let you know. Take the opportunity to zone out and do some meditation. Things will hot up in about…' a quick consult with his watch '…thirty minutes.'

Chapter Twenty-Nine

19:35, Tuesday 13 March

THE INTERIOR of the Ford Transit was charged with pent-up energy, the only sounds – focused breathing, the shuffle of boots on the floor of the van and the rustle of clothing. From outside came moans of wind and occasional gull squawks. The heavy vehicle rocked slightly from side to side as if it wasn't on land at all, but another vessel out on the sea. Light was fading by the minute, until the point where visibility inside the van reduced to almost nothing. The glow-in-the-dark hands on Jack's watch told him in two minutes nautical twilight would be over.

All Jack's senses were heightened, he could almost distinguish who was wearing what cologne. Adrenaline pumped through every fibre, nerve endings twitched. Could the others hear his heart, furiously beating inside his ribcage? Chesterfield banged the heel of his fist against the side of the van, everyone jumped in their seats. 'Almost show time, folks. Remember your roles, OK?'

All officers, now looking like green Martians via the phosphorescent image intensification screen in Jack's night vision goggles, nodded vigorously.

'Stay as low as you can, communicate with each other using hand signals when you can, over the headsets with discretion. OK. Move!'

Islington pushed open the rear door, the cops spilled out, hit the ground like paratroopers jumping out of a plane. Jack aligned himself next to Chesterfield, glad to be paired up with the experienced commander. The officers clambered over a low rock wall, dropped to a crouch and began trotting in a north-westerly direction towards the house, 278 metres distant. The blustery wind had eased to around 20 knots and was now blowing into the officers' backs. The rain had reduced to a thick mist. Shit night for a stroll, perfect for a rescue operation.

The team maintained a relatively straight line across the field – Jack could only see Chesterfield to his right and Khan five metres or so to his left. Up ahead, the unkempt stone house, bathed in its own eery green light through the goggles, loomed like a spectre from a gothic horror novel. Puffs of smoke emerged from a chimney pot on the far side of the house only to be dissipated by the wind almost instantly. There were three other chimneys on the house, however no smoke emanated from them. Fingers crossed the house contained only the three men the neighbour had observed. And Skye.

Now, they were only 100 metres from the house. Jack could feel his heart hammering like a pneumatic drill. He squinted through his goggles and made out the contours and windows of the southern façade. No lights were switched on on this side of the house, although the image enhancement revealed some illumination coming through a window or perhaps door glass on the western side.

Chesterfield silently sprinted ahead ten metres, turned and motioned for everyone to drop to the ground. In a prone position in a cold, dark field of wet grass and thistles, Jack's resolve tempered like steel. The was the most important job in his entire life. He repeated the mantra: *failure is not an option!* If he had to sacrifice his own life to save Skye, so be it.

The commander conducted another soundcheck. His voice came loud and clear through Jack's headset. All confirmed they could hear him. 'Please activate body cams to gather evidence and to protect your own arses. Done? OK. Await my signal to proceed.' Jack watched as Chesterfield plucked a wireless alarm jammer from his backpack, placed it on the ground and turned it on. 'OK. Move!'

The designated pairs commando-crawled towards one of the four facades of the two-storey house: O'Toole and Pedersen were to take the north side (kitchen and lower floor bathroom); Jessop and Khan – west (two bedrooms, one lower and one upper floor); Harper and Islington – south (laundry and woodshed, lower floor); Chesterfield and Jack – east (reception room lower floor, bedroom and bathroom upper floor).

Jack struggled for air, working hard to traverse the distance laden with so much equipment. Every metre hurt, but he didn't care. *Press on.* Then, a tap on the forearm and a held-up hand from Chesterfield made him stop. They'd reached a point approximately fifty metres from the eastern side of the building. In quick succession, three voices came over the headset, saying three words. *In position, over.* Chesterfield informed the others that he and Jack were also now in position, ordered them to deploy their ultra-sensitive listening devices for five minutes and await further commands. He then produced his MI5-engineered laser microphone and sensor, as well as a separate smaller headset, pointed the mic at the closed double casement window on the upper floor. His mouth twisted in concentration, tongue poking out, while he fiddled with dials and switches; Jack assumed he was running calibrations. A single light lit up on the handle of the microphone and a row of lights on the sensor flashed until they all glowed solid. The commander half-grinned at Jack and gave a thumbs up. Chesterfield then donned the second headset while holding the mic in his outstretched arm towards the window on the second floor. Officers would be doing the exact same thing on the other sides of the house.

Jack could barely keep still, desperate to ask the commander *Are you getting anything? Can you hear her?* But all he could do was wait. After what seemed an age, the commander removed the small headset. He nodded his head slowly, but his lips were pressed together in a thin line.

'What?' said Jack.

'From the window on the left I'm detecting what could be human sounds, possibly whining or moaning, but gosh, it's hard to tell. Could be a leaky tap from the adjoining bathroom echoing in the bedroom.' He pointed at the window on the right. 'We'll have to give it another go, see if we pick up something conclusive before making any further decisions.'

That wasn't dodgy plumbing, thought Jack. What Chesterfield heard *had* to be Skye. He glanced at his watch. 19:50. Only ten minutes before the deadline ticked over. 'Can I listen? I'll recognise her better than you can.'

Before Chesterfield could answer, a response came back from Harper. *Negative.* Immediately after that a second response, from Jessop. *Negative.* Then O'Toole. *Positive!* Jack's pulse quickened. 'I can clearly hear three different male voices behind the window I'm targeting,' she reported. 'They seem excited, I heard sounds like clinking bottles or glasses, laughter. I'm not able to make out what they're saying. But right now, they're all together in the kitchen. It's a small room, only a couple of square metres.'

'Excellent work, DC O'Toole,' said Chesterfield. 'According to the old house plan, there's a short corridor running from the kitchen leading to a flight of stairs up to the second floor. Now, if you—'

Without waiting to hear the rest of what Chesterfield had to say, Jack grabbed the smaller headset from the ground, put it on, then pointed the microphone at the upstairs bedroom window. What he heard was exactly as Chesterfield described. The sounds were indeterminate, but even if Jack's ears refused to confirm it was Skye, his gut told him the truth. He ripped the headset off, handed it back to the commander, who was still conversing with O'Toole.

'Roger that. One moment.' Chesterfield muted his mic, ripped of his comms headset and glared at Jack. 'What… the hell…are you doing?'

'It's her up there. I swear on my life. We have to get her out now before they realise we're here! The second they clock us, one of 'em will be up there with a knife to her throat. They had no compunction killing an innocent man if you recall.'

'Listen, calm down,' Chesterfield hissed. 'I don't need to tell you, one false step and it could be…'

Jack wasn't listening. There was a small clapboard shed, most of the timbers rotting or missing. Perhaps there was a ladder in there. He stood to make a run for it, but Chesterfield had him around the waist in a standing rugby tackle. The man's grip was vicelike and Jack was going nowhere. 'Stop! It was a mistake bringing you along. I told Calthorpe he was a fool for allowing it.'

Damn this toffee-nosed twit. Jack summoned all his strength to wrestle free of the man's hold, spun around to face him. 'You're the fool! We've got them in the palm of our hands right now. It's time to act. Tell O'Toole and Pedersen to bust the door down with the others to follow. Chuck in a handful of those stun-grenades. We've got a couple of assault rifles, for fuck's sake!'

'But we have no idea what they've got in there. Could be a whole arsenal of weapons!'

How thick could this bloke be? 'Now it's your turn to listen to me. You might be a flaming hero when it comes to the obstacle course and playing soldiers, but I know what goes on in a criminal's head!' Jack jabbed at his own temple with a forefinger. 'Trust me. I understand these people. Skye's up there in that room, probably gagged and tied, cold and starving. Let me at least see if there's something I can use to climb up to that window and–'

'Enough!' Chesterfield pinched the bridge of his nose. 'My training's telling me to wait, but if your gut tells you that's your daughter making those sounds, then it probably is.' He paused, clearly weighing up his options. 'But if she's downstairs with the kidnappers and you're wrong…'

'I'm not fucking wrong!'

Chesterfield pointed at his chest. 'Just remember, this body cam's recording everything, and so is yours. Swear to me, Lisbon, that the sound you heard is Skye and you're willing to stake the success of the operation on your word.'

'Yeah. I'm willing to stake everything. In my professional opinion, we can take those clowns out in a heartbeat with zero casualties on our side.' Jack bent low and stared into the lens of Chesterfield's body cam. 'And if it all goes pear shaped, I'll take the heat.'

Chapter Thirty

19:48, Tuesday 13 March

THE CRAMPED ROOM, windows shut tight against the wind and rain, stank of fried fish, boiled cabbage and cigarette smoke. Greasy enamel plates, china cups, glasses and cutlery were piled high in the steel sink, stained here and there where teabags had been squeezed and left to dry. A green plastic chopping board on the kitchen bench showed the smudged vestiges of a line of cocaine.

The three men had been sitting around a battered old wooden table, drinking, smoking, taking the odd snort of blow, and watching the clock for two hours. It was now 19:48. A laptop was open, logged onto McNair's brand-new cryptocurrency account. The balance of zero would soon skyrocket to 20 Bitcoin, worth well in excess of £600,000.

'D'ya reckon we can book our flights to Hawaii tonight boss, or should we wait till tomorrow?' Alistair Gordon poured himself a finger of whisky, slammed it down and reached for a yellow half-litre can of Tennent's lager. He burped loudly, stood from the kitchen table and edged to the front of the open fire, turning his backside towards the flames.

'Oi. We're all feeling the cold, mate,' said Brinkworth. 'Have some manners and get out the way of the fire, you selfish prick.'

The ex-soldier shook a fist. 'Don't be getting all indignant with me, pal. If you'd bothered to chop some wood like I asked you instead of watching telly all day, ya lazy bastard, we wouldnae be—'

McNair tapped a grimy fingernail on the table. 'Come on, fellas. It's just one more night in this shitbox, then we all go home.' He turned to Gordon. 'Besides, aren't you supposed to be a tough ex-military man? A bit of cold shouldn't bother you.'

'Aye,' Gordon laughed. 'But I was trained to endure the blazing heat of the Middle East, not this freezing dump.'

McNair laughed, Brinkworth offered a begrudging smile.

'Listen.' McNair doubled clicked a wireless mouse, scribbled something in a notepad, adjusted his glasses and looked back at the screen. 'I think we should send Detective Lisbon a wee photo of his lassie. He must be terribly worried. I'd like to alleviate his concerns.' He looked up at Gordon. 'Since you're so miserable frae the cold, how about you pop up and take a snap. The exercise will warm you up.' He opened up the back of an older model mobile phone and inserted a new SIM card, closed it up again. 'And take her up a piece of that delicious trout. I'm no meanie.'

'There's none left,' said Brinkworth flatly, lighting a cigarette and inhaling deeply. 'Soldier boy ate the last of it.

We'd have to scale, clean and cook another one. And I ain't volunteering for that job again.'

'Oh dear,' said McNair. 'Never mind. She can have another dry cracker, I suppose.' He handed Gordon the phone. 'Hurry up about it. I want to send the photo to him right after the Bitcoins land.'

Gordon snatched the phone with a frown, stomped down the corridor, grabbed the loose banister rail and headed up the stairs. At the top, he turned left, tapped on the door. 'Ready for a fashion shoot?' he called out in his cheeriest voice. Then he gave himself a mental head slap. She was restrained and couldn't answer anyway. Must be the booze addling his mind. He'd made a promise to himself to stay away from it, but when in the company of other drinkers it was hard to resist. Even more so when you have to tolerate a tosser like Brinkworth. He was some distant relative of McNair's, but that's a poor reason to hire someone to do important work. Driving a van, yeah, he could do that well enough. But as for other talents, he was useless.

Gordon turned on the mobile's camera app. A couple of photos from different angles and the boss could choose the best one to send. He turned the doorhandle, stepped across the threshold, fumbled around with his left hand for the light switch.

Something doesn't feel right in here. He should have heard silence, at most the soft breathing of the kid. Instead came the sound of a howling wind and the guttural cry of a very angry man.

Chapter Thirty-One

19:55, Tuesday 13 March

THE WIND KEPT PLAYING its capricious games. From a strong breeze half an hour ago it had increased to around 30 knots – a near gale on the Beaufort scale – with needles of rain for good measure. Chesterfield crouched low while Jack stood on the commander's wobbling shoulders. A flex of the knees and Jack was standing tall like a man on stilts. He stretched out his hand for the window ledge, clawing fingers fell tantalisingly short. If he could curl a couple of fingers over the ledge, he had enough strength to hang on with one hand while swinging the handle of the Glock with the other and break the glass. Then he could haul himself in, probably sustaining cuts but he couldn't care less about that. *One more try.* Like a baseballer facing up to a pitcher, he wriggled his feet on Chesterfield's shoulders for better purchase, stood on his tiptoes, extending every tendon in his feet till they burned. *Still, a fraction shy of the mark.*

'You got it?' said Chesterfield, craning his chin up the side of the wall.

'No, dammit.'

'Feels like you're going to tumble off.'

'Quick, let me down. I've got an idea.'

Back on solid ground, Jack lumbered through the slanting rain to the rickety wooden structure next to the house. There had to be something in there he could use, maybe he could stack some hay bales. Then, in the corner…an old wooden pallet. *Yes.* He picked it up by the middle strut and carried it back to Chesterfield. Jack flipped the pallet on its side, the palings effectively rungs on a ladder. He wedged it hard against the wall at the steepest angle he could without losing stability. The men repeated their initial acrobat manoeuvre, before Chesterfield ascended the pallet with Jack on his shoulders, gripping the stones on the wall for balance.

When Chesterfield had climbed up the pallet as far as he could, Jack's eyes, blinking constantly to squeeze out the rain, were just able to see through the window. *There she is!* Her face glowed bright green in his goggles. *Is she sick with fever?* Jack's heart ached to see her bound and gagged. At the same time a burning hate for the perpetrators drove him on. Possessed of a demonic strength, he gripped the barrel of the Glock, roared like a wild man. He took a mighty swing and the pane of glass shattered. He bent down and yelled at Chesterfield, 'Once I'm inside, give the command to the others.'

JACK CLAMBERED TO HIS FEET, brushed shards of glass off his body. *Get the ties and gag off her!*

Not yet.

Another pair of eyes glowed green inside the bedroom like some radioactive zombie. He was a big man, bigger than Jack by half a head and built like a brick shithouse. Jack recognised the features from the CCTV footage. *He doesn't know I'm here.* Jack racked the slide of the Glock at the precise moment the overhead light clicked on. He raised his gun with two hands and aimed it squarely at the man's forehead. 'Nice to meet you, Mr McTaggart. I mean Gordon. Now…' Before he could get the words out, two loud bangs and police officers shouting unintelligible words echoed up the stairwell. Jack screamed '…GET ON THE GROUND NOW OR I'LL BLOW YOUR FUCKING BRAINS OUT!'

The big ox meekly obeyed. Jack stomped over and delivered a ripping kick into Gordon's kidney, steel toecaps first. The thug cried out in agony. 'Why aren't your hands interlocked behind your head?' said Jack, giving the man another kick on the other side. Gordon thrashed about on the floor, screamed again.

'Because…you didn't…ah…ask…me to.'

'Nobody likes a smart arse.' A third kick for luck brought another cry of pain. Jack dropped his knee squarely into the back of the man's neck. 'With your military training, I thought you'd be smart enough to surrender properly to a superior force.' Jack applied snap ties around the man's wrists, pulled them tight. He bent close to Gordon's ear. 'And I'll tell you this, sunshine. If there weren't seven other cops downstairs dealing with your mates and the trauma it would cause my daughter, I'd empty the magazine into your brain right now.' Jack stood, applied ties around the man's ankles. There'd be some fallout from the body cam evidence of him slipping the boot in, but he'd deal with that later. Maybe Pedersen could help make it disappear.

He ripped off the annoying helmet and goggles, extracted the knife from his utility belt. He couldn't resist the temptation, dug the point of it into the skin next to a pulsating vein in Gordon's neck, pushed until a droplet of blood appeared. 'By the way, I'm figuring you for the murder of the ice-cream man. You're fucked!'

Skye's moans grew louder. With the threat well and truly neutralised, he sat down beside her, touched her cheek. She was frozen stiff. He'd have to wrap her up in an aluminium thermal blanket ASAP. And get her a warm drink and something to eat. He slit Skye's bonds, released the gag and pulled her close to his chest, hugged her like he'd never see her again. Her cold forehead pressed against his cheek as he whispered nonsensical worlds of comfort into her ear. She pulled away, gazed at him with a crazed look in her eyes, pupils shrinking quickly as they grew accustomed to the light. Then, the confusion lifted from her face as she recognised him. She broke into a lopsided smile, stuttering something incomprehensible. Jack asked her to repeat it.

'Hey, Daddy.'

'Yes, honey?'

'I knew you'd come for me.'

DOWNSTAIRS IT LOOKED like a small bomb had gone off. Upturned furniture, smashed crockery, the side door to the kitchen hanging off one hinge and splinters scattered across the threshold. Residual smoke from the flashbangs competed with the stink of other domestic smells and the unwashed bodies of two pathetic criminals. McNair, tufts of sparse brown hair jutting in all directions, sat in one of the kitchen chairs, arms tied behind his back – his accomplice, name unknown to Jack, in another. Chesterfield, Pedersen and O'Toole stood guard while Jack carried Skye into a small reception room past the rear of the kitchen. Once there, he sat her on a battered fabric sofa and draped a thermal blanket around her shoulders. The shivering was less severe now, warmth returning to her face and hands. Jack returned to the kitchen, fetched a cup of hot tea with milk and four sugars and a packet of sweet biscuits from a cupboard under the sink. 'Eat all of them if you like.' He gave his daughter a cuddle and vowed to be back again soon. She smiled and nodded, the ordeal somehow affecting her less than Jack had feared. But he was under no illusion – there would be trauma to deal with later.

Jack stormed into the kitchen, lasered his focus on McNair. The man had changed significantly since the photo of him holidaying on Sanday taken a decade ago. He'd put on at least twenty pounds and his hair had thinned out. Flabby and pasty faced, the man was a pitiful specimen. Jack picked a chair up off the floor, spun it around and sat on it backwards. 'I figure it's your lucky day, Donald. Lucky in the sense you weren't riddled with bullets by my colleagues.' A blue and purple welt bloomed under McNair's eye and blood dripped from a small cut to his forehead. 'You'll soon be on your way back to...' He turned to Chesterfield. '...where the hell are we taking them?'

'Kirkwall Police Station. They'll spend the night there until we can transfer them back to London tomorrow. The kidnapping and the murder were committed there, so they'll serve prison sentences in England.'

'Prison? Murder? You've not even charged us with

anything,' said the unknown man, a jittery skinny bloke with a dodgy hipster haircut and beard.

'Shut up, moron. No one was talking to you.' Jack turned back to McNair. 'The thing I wanna know is *why*, mate? Why target us of all people? I don't understand it.'

'You killed Gallagher and stole millions from him. I figured you could spare a measly £600,000 or so worth of crypto.' The man's words were defiant, but the way his bottom lip turned down at the edges and quivered told another story.

'First of all, I never offed Gallagher. But whoever it was that did, you should be grateful to 'em. That no-good arsehole killed *your* father, for fuck's sake.'

McNair shrugged. 'No comment. I want my lawyer.'

'You're gonna have to wait. But not even Perry bloody Mason could get you off. Too much evidence, dickhead.'

Chesterfield wedged himself between Jack and McNair. 'Sorry to interrupt your wee conversation, Detective Lisbon. It's already 20:30, and we have to make tracks. Jessop's brought the van to take us to Loth Pier. There'll be a boat coming for us in half an hour. The rest of the team are already there waiting for us.'

Jack stood, stabbed a finger at McNair. 'Lucky for you it's time to go. I was fixing on rearranging your features while Detective Chesterfield here looked the other way. In fact, I think I will anyway.' Jack spat on his palms and rubbed them together, then cocked his right fist. McNair closed his eyes and let out a squeal. 'Ha ha. Only kidding, mate. You'll get yours in prison. Abductors of kids aren't the most popular inmates. Your life inside will be a living hell.' He turned to fetch Skye, then decided he wanted a parting word with McNair. 'You know something, your dad Angus was an effin' legend about town. I used to watch old videos of his fights. An honourable and honest man, by all accounts. You, on the other hand, are a complete and utter loser.'

McNair stared down at the table, refused to make eye contact.

'You know why I think that? Besides you getting caught so easy, that is.'

McNair shrugged.

'Those Bitcoins you were so excited about? The transaction was totally fake. Outsmarted and outgunned. You're a waste of space.' He spat on the floor and went to get his daughter.

The son of the legendary boxer Angus MacNair dropped his head forward and sobbed uncontrollably. His accomplice could only stare into space.

Chapter Thirty-Two

10:55, Thursday 15 March

THE SALON BUZZED with furious activity, the constant snip, snip, snip of scissors blending with the buzz of hairdryers and light-hearted conversation. The heady scents of nail polish, ammonia from hair dyes, the sweetness of shampoos and conditioners and the eye-watering clouds of hairspray competed with the rich aroma of coffee percolating in a glass pot. The normal atmosphere in Pharoah's Hair and Nails. Today, however, was a train wreck. Newbie apprentice Brandi had created chaos after she misunderstood the appointment book and scheduled a number of clients for the same time. Now the employees could barely keep pace. All four chairs facing the huge wall mirrors were occupied by customers. A pair of middle-aged women sat on the sofa, blathering on about last night's episode of *The Real Housewives of Cheshire* while they waited their turn. Other regulars had left in a huff after learning they'd have to wait an extra ninety minutes or more for their appointment.

Sarah felt an insistent vibration in the pocket of her smock. It was rude to answer the phone mid-haircut, especially with the salon in damage control, but she had a fair idea who was on the other end and she needed to vent.

She listened to his apology without interruption. Until he made the outlandish request. The man must have lost all sense of reality. 'Sorry, I think I must've misheard you.' Sarah rolled her eyes to the accompaniment of a sarcastic laugh. 'I thought you said you wanted to see your daughter again.'

'That's exactly what I said.'

Sarah realised this conversation would take more than a couple of minutes, took a step back from the woman in the chair and held a hand over the phone. 'Will you excuse me while I take this call in private, luv? Won't be a minute.' She flashed the elderly customer a trademark hundred-watt smile.

The wrinkled, blue-rinsed old woman grinned back, nodded understandingly. 'Take your time, dear. I ain't in no hurry.'

In the alley at the back of the salon Sarah sat on an upturned milk crate, lit a menthol cigarette with one hand while holding her phone with the other. She gave her head a side to side shake, flicked her hair defiantly even though there was no one to see it. 'I shouldn't be wastin' my precious breath on you, Jack Lisbon, but I'm due for a laugh, so go on.'

'It's partly your fault the whole thing happened, you know.'

She took a long drag and almost spat the smoke out. He was pathetic. 'Oh is it, now? That's rich. You were supposed to have your eyes on her the whole time, not go chasin' damsels in distress who turned out to be, what do they call it these days? Oh yeah, fake news!'

'Come on, Sarah. There was only one way the kidnappers had the drop on us. You let the cat out of the bag by blabbing to Phoebe about where me and Skye were going. Then she told her brother who passed the information on and next thing—'

'Oh, so it's a crime these days to talk about your family, is it?' She stood, began to pace the cobblestones. 'In my experience, it's normal to chat with your workmates about what your kids are up to. I'm a proud mum, understand? I know you're a useless piece of shite, but for reasons unknown the public's got this idea that you're some kind of hero. Just for doing the job you get paid to do! People don't think I'm a hero for styling their hair or polishing their nails, do they?'

'Well, I...ah...maybe they should. You deserve...' He mumbled something else incoherent; she didn't even ask him to repeat it.

She glanced up at the sky as an aeroplane jetted off somewhere. What a pity Jack wasn't on that plane going back to Australia. He still had a couple of weeks to spend in the UK before returning home. Bad luck for him, but he'd have to amuse himself without Skye.

'I bet you don't get flustered like a fool when you're roughing up suspects, do you? You can't speak properly with me because you have a guilty conscience. My poor baby's gonna be having nightmares the rest of her life because of your negligence. And she'll probably have to give evidence in court. Which will only lead to her reliving the ordeal. So, no. I'm afraid you will not be seeing her again. EVER!'

'Come on, be reasonable. We got her back safe and

sound and caught a gang of murderous criminals into the bargain.'

'Can you even hear yourself? That poor old man only got killed because YOU abandoned your post at the critical moment. At least that's what the police officers told me when they delivered Skye to me.'

'That's unfair and you know it. Kids have to have some independence. It's impossible to watch them all the time. What about when Skye's at school? You can't monitor her then, can you? And...yes, that's right...she told me she takes the bus to school all by herself.'

If Jack was here right now, Sarah would slap his face. Skye adored the man, even after he put her life in danger, but enough was enough. 'She's safer at school or on a bus – or anywhere for that matter – than she could ever be in your company.'

'Where is she now? Surely she's not back at school yet.'

'Of course she's not at school, you idiot! She's at my mother's place. The doctor said she needs two weeks off – two weeks of her education she can't afford to miss – then, wait for it, monthly sessions with a psychologist until an assessment determines she's recovered. That could be years!'

Phoebe stuck her head out the back door, saw Sarah was in no mood for a friendly chat, dashed back inside. She'd confessed to Sarah she felt tremendous guilt that she'd told her brother things he didn't need to know. Sarah found it easy to forgive Phoebe – in fact there was nothing to forgive. How was she to know Elrod was on the payroll of a maniac? Her current problem, though, was the man on the other end of the phone line. She ploughed on, determined to get the message through his thick skull. 'So let's get one thing clear. You attract trouble like shit attracts flies. If not for you coming back to town, none of this would have happened.' She sucked in a deep drag that almost burned the cigarette down to the butt. 'Furthermore, you lied to me about going to, where was it? Oh yeah, fucking Cornwall! And I, like an idiot, believed you. All the while some psychos have dragged her off to Scotland. Damn it, mon, I just can't take your crap anymore. Don't call again. Goodbye.' She disconnected the call, crushed out the cigarette with a twist of her heel, wiped her hands on her apron and stormed back into the salon.

THE URGE TO leap from the wagon of sobriety had wrenched at Jack's brain many times since he took his last drink of alcohol three years ago. Each time the temptation had reared its ugly head he'd managed to resist. Tonight, with the chance to be with his daughter gone for good, that urge was pulling like the world-champion tug-of-war team. Still, he would resist again.

'What'll it be?' asked the barman with a complete lack of interest. Jack stared at the man's profile as he eyeballed an attractive blonde on the far side of the small restaurant bar.

'A rum and a coke.'

'Sorry, I missed that.' The man stopped ogling the woman, who had turned to kiss a short bald man who looked twice her age. The barman diligently wiped a non-existent spillage from the highly polished wooden bar top. 'What did you say you're having? Scotch and coke?'

'If you paid more attention to customers instead of drooling over women like a disgusting pervert you'd have heard me.' Jack gave the bloke his best Billy Idol sneer. 'I said a rum and a coke.' Jack double tapped a finger on the bar.

'A rum and coke coming up.'

'No, sunshine. Listen, for fuck's sake. I'll say it slowly for you. One rum, one coke. Two drinks, in separate glasses.'

The pony-tailed man gave a tiny shrug, a few moments later returning with the drinks and a packet of pork scratchings, Jack figured by way of an apology for being a pratt. The pretentious eatery in an upmarket part of Chelsea was the type of establishment Jack hated. After five years in tropical northern Australia he had come to prefer laid-back, working-class pubs. But DCI Lars Pedersen had offered to pick up the tab, so he wasn't arguing.

A light tap on the elbow. Pedersen was dressed immaculately in a slim-fit dark blue suit with matching tie. He smelled like he'd spilled half a bottle of expensive aftershave on himself. 'You're early.'

'Yeah, well.' Jack tossed a handful of the salty snack into his mouth. 'I ain't got nowhere else to be. I'm cutting my holiday short.'

'Why?'

'Why do you think? I came all this way for one reason and one reason only. To spend time with my daughter. As you're well aware, it all went tits up and now Sarah's blocking access.'

'You can challenge that through the courts. You've got rights.'

'You might be a smart copper, Lars, but you don't know this woman. She'll dig her heels in. Besides, Skye doesn't need the extra drama. I'm totally gutted.'

Pedersen draped a comradely arm around Jack's shoulder. 'None of this is your fault.'

Jack grabbed his glass of coke and pointed it towards an

empty booth. Pedersen ordered an Asahi beer before the two men slid onto shiny orange bench seats, edged close to the wall away from prying ears and eyes.

'I think you left your other drink behind,' said Pedersen.

'Yeah. I always order an alcoholic drink and leave it sitting on the bar. It's become a ritual. A test of my sobriety.'

The two men maintained a pensive silence for a minute before Jack had to ask. 'What happens next?'

'We interview McNair and Gordon again. See if we can make them crack and confess to the murder. There's no getting out of the kidnapping charge with video and a squadron of cops as witnesses, and the murder should be easy enough to prove to a jury. But as you know, confessions make our job so much easier.'

'True.' The old Jack would have beaten a confession out of them without a second thought. 'What about that third bloke?'

'Glen Brinkworth. A second cousin of McNair's. From what we can gather, his role was nothing more than driving the vehicle and doing odd jobs. He'll still get a stiff sentence after the trial, though.'

Jack stirred a melting ice cube with his finger. 'And the woman? Have you tracked her down?'

'Yeah. Suzie Field. She's been working for McNair for a couple of years now. He hired her as a bookkeeper, but with some extra-curricular activities thrown in. She's been holding up under questioning, but something tells me she'll be the first rat to desert the sinking ship.'

'What do you mean by extra-curricular activities? Don't tell me she was sleeping with that creep?' Jack couldn't credit it, but money was often a motivator for people to do the most distasteful acts.

'I don't know about that. I was talking about running errands for him. And of course, the diversion in the park.'

'Oh, right.' That made more sense.

'We picked her up after raiding McNair's home in East Kilbride. She was in the middle of restocking his drinks cabinet. He's a big fan of Kahlua, apparently. Anyway, she's in remand like the rest of the scum. After yesterday's press conference with photos of all the perps, a couple of witnesses have already come forward.'

'I think I know who some of them will be.' Jack took a slug of his coke, placed the glass back on the coaster softly, like it was made of plastic explosives. 'I've got a couple more questions, if you don't mind.'

'Fire away.'

'Do you have any idea how they got my old UK phone number to contact me in the first place? My *private* number. It's been bothering me the whole time.'

'We're not sure at this stage, but we have a theory. Their lawyer's told them not to say anything and they're heeding his advice. But I got O'Toole to do some digging. It turns out Alistair Gordon used to work with another bloke called Mark Halbert. They served together in—'

'In the effing Highlanders Battalion!' It was coming back. Fifteen years ago, but now clear as day. 'After a brief stint in the army, Mark decided to become a cop. We went to Hendon academy together. He was a salt-of-the-Earth kinda guy. We shared a room.'

'That's right. O'Toole joined the dots between you and the two of them. Sadly, after Halbert left the Met and joined the Scottish police force he turned as bent as a three-bob banknote.'

'I hadn't heard about that.' Jack remembered Halbert as an honest and generous man with a fierce determination to see criminals punished. They were all idealistic in their naïve youth. But out in the real world, surrounded by temptation, many turned bad. Including Jack. Difference was, Jack got offered an opportunity to make good and he'd grabbed it with both hands.

'Halbert's currently serving the first year of a seven-year sentence for corruption. He took backhanders from Glasgow drug gangs to turn a blind eye. A shame. By all accounts he was an outstanding officer early in his career.'

Jack rubbed his forehead. Halbert had been his best friend at the academy. They sparred together, gone out drinking together, chased women together. Even if he had been corrupt, that didn't mean sharing the phone number was a malicious act. Perhaps Gordon was clever enough to get him to hand it over without arousing suspicion. Gordon aka McTaggart had also leaned on someone else to get the jump on Jack. 'Elrod Smart.'

'What about him?'

'What has he told you?'

'Plenty. His evidence could be crucial in making the murder charge stick. In conjunction with physical evidence. At the murder scene we retrieved fibres from clothing that we're confident of tying to Gordon. It's just a matter of waiting for the lab results.' Pedersen pulled a pair of reading glasses from his top pocket. 'Ready to order?'

'We haven't finished with Smart. I'll tell you something, sunshine, if I had him alone in the interview room he'd be feeling plenty of heat.'

Pedersen raised a hand. 'Be kind, mate. The lad's got emotional problems. He's told us what made him do it. Gordon offered him a hundred quid to ask his sister about what you were up to. Plus the threat of a bashing if he didn't co-operate.'

'I shouldn't be too hard on the lad. I did give him a pasting myself all those years ago.'

'Indeed.' Pedersen brushed a speck of lint from his trousers. 'And he's fully on board to give evidence.'

'Speaking of which, the body cam stuff...'

'Hmm. The camera you wore somehow failed to record anything, but everyone else's seemed to work fine.'

'Funny that,' said Jack, giving his old friend a knowing smile. 'Technology can be so temperamental, hey?'

'Indeed.'

'Look. Do you think there'll be a chance of Skye not having to testify?'

Pedersen nodded. 'Every chance. I'll push as hard as I can to keep her out of it. If we can't nail them without her testimony, we can ensure it's given via a recording or remote live link to keep her out of the court.'

'Can you make sure Sarah understands that? She won't talk to me and I'd like her not to worry unduly.'

'Sure. Hungry yet?'

'I guess I could eat.' Jack studied the menu, not liking any of the unpronounceable offerings. He decided to let Pedersen order for him. 'What can you tell me about McNair himself? His dad was a hero of mine back in the day. I can't believe the fruit of his loins could turn out to be such an arsehole.'

A waiter came, cleared the empty glasses and took their dinner order. Pedersen recommended a filet mignon with seasonal vegetables, promised Jack he wouldn't be disappointed. Over their meal, which, Jack had to admit to himself, was spectacular, the DCI gave Jack a summary of McNair's life. High-school graduate but no further education. In and out of youth custody centres as a teenager, lost the plot after his dad died in the ring. He developed an online gambling business which was largely successful, earning him tens of thousands a month. His long-term drug addiction – specifically cocaine – had seen him acquire a string of fines over the years, but somehow he'd avoided jail. Lately his business was losing money hand over fist to smarter competitors from Eastern Europe. As for his targeting of Jack, Pedersen said, 'No doubt McNair junior believed the crazy rumours you killed Alex Gallagher and made off with a fortune. Unbelievable, huh?' Pedersen gave a chuckle, stabbed a piece of chicken breast and looked at Jack with a slightly tilted head and a half-closed eye.

Christ, thought Jack. *He knows!*

'SO THEY RECKON you won't have to testify, guv?' shouted Sheehan, unsteadily placing on the table a tray of three foaming pints of Guinness, a shot glass of rum and a standard coke with ice. 'That's good news, innit?'

The throbbing 1980s punk music – playlist organised by Micky Knox – that blasted inside the Mare's Head pub made normal conversation impossible. Jack leaned forward to speak, the other men leaned forward to listen. 'There's been no court date set for either the murder or the kidnapping matters. Pedersen told me there's a backlog of cases in the courts of more than six months. Add to that the time McNair and Gordon's lawyers need to build a defense and it's clear there won't be a trial anytime soon. Any appearance by me would be via video link from Australia.'

Bruiser raised his glass. 'I'd say not having to testify in court was damned good news. Not in the same league as rescuing a little girl, but good news all the same. Here's to an unlikely bunch of crime stoppers. To us!'

Jack, Sheehan and a beaming Micky Knox followed suit. 'To us!'

'To be fair,' said Jack. 'If Micky hadn't made the decision to follow Elrod here, had a word with Eric the Red and made the connection between the gym and that prick Donald McNair, we wouldn't be sitting here right now.'

The men agreed that, yes, Micky deserved a special mention, but it was a team effort and, after all, who was it but Jack who sat the kidnapper on his arse? Another toast. *To Jack!*

More pints were drunk, crisps eaten, jokes told. Jack was content to nurse his coke, now warm and flat.

Despite the self-congratulation, the smugness of victory, joy was tinged with sadness. Jack had revealed that Sarah was refusing to let him see Skye under any circumstances. He vowed to keep trying to get through, but as far as this trip went, the chances of Sarah relenting were slim to none. Therefore, he'd be flying out within the next two days. The lads offered soothing words of sympathy, but no matter how much they tried to cheer him up, Jack had to force every smile, every laugh.

One of Jack's all-time favourite pieces of punk genius poured through the speakers. The title summed up his feelings perfectly. "Pretty Vacant". He banged his head in time to the music, sensing a building urge to pogo dance around the crowded bar, smashing into punters and not giving a toss if he upset anyone. Perhaps even start a fight.

But for that to happen, he'd need a drink.

Something to dull the senses and numb the pain. A strong, fiery drink like vodka, something The Sex Pistols would approve of. Yeah, fuck it. No doubt he'd regret this decision later, but now was now, and tomorrow was a hundred years in the future. About as long as he'd have to wait to ever see his kid again.

When the hypnotic guitar of "Hong Kong Garden" by Siouxsie and the Banshees kicked in, Jack made his move. Younger people were digging the new-wave classic they'd probably never heard in their lives, thrashing and leaping about. Jack weaved, ducked and sidestepped his way to the bar.

Double vodka in hand, he threaded his way back to the group. Bruiser had gone home, Sheehan was nodding like a drowsy bird, about to fall head-first into his pint, and Knox was already sleeping, his head resting on the back of his hands. Before addressing the chilled vodka, Jack decided to quickly check online for available flights to Brisbane. Better to lock one in now than get totally wasted – which was looming as a distinct possibility – and miss out on a good deal. He fished out his phone, typed the password and did an immediate double take. *What the…?*

He might be banned from contacting Sarah, but the same rules didn't apply to her. Four missed calls and a couple of messages. He listened to the latest message and broke into a huge smile. He stood, drank the remains of the warm coke, tipped the vodka into Sheehan's pint glass and strode out into the brisk night air.

Chapter Thirty-Three

'IS DETECTIVE CLAUDIA TAYLOR YOUR GIRLFRIEND?' said Skye, nonchalantly picking up a card from the deck. Without waiting for an answer she took a sip of milk, nibbled the end of a chocolate biscuit and studied her cards.

Where the hell did that one come from? 'Excuse me?' said Jack. 'I'm trying to concentrate on the game. Now you've thrown me off completely.' He placed his cards face down on the table, frowned and shook his head. 'That's dirty tactics!'

Skye shot her father one of those stares only children are capable of. Daring you to lie. 'Are you boyfriend and girlfriend? Mum reckons you and DC Taylor are, what did she call it? Oh yeah, an item. Is that true?'

Jack stared back at her. 'No, we are not an item. We are indeed, two items. I am me and she is…she.'

'Hmm.' Skye looked at her cards again, pointed at them one by one, her lips moving as she counted in her head. 'I wouldn't blame you for liking her, actually. I've seen videos of her answering questions at those press thingies, and she's awesome. You got a…six?'

'Go fish.' Jack scratched his head in wonder. The child had undergone an ordeal that would have finished off many an adult. Yet this one behaved as if it never happened. Not only that, Skye had manipulated her mother so expertly that now Jack's presence in her life was not undesirable, it was essential. 'You got a Queen?'

'Yes.' She stood up from her chair, twirled and gave a royal wave. 'Me!'

'And I'm the Joker, I suppose.'

'No!' She raced around to the opposite side of the round kitchen table and wrapped her arms around his neck. 'You're the King, daddy.'

Last night he was one shot glass away from being a dead beat, now he was a king. The bolt-from-the-blue message from his ex had read as follows. I don't know what you said to that girl, but she's threatening to go on a hunger strike if I don't let her see you. She's already missed four meals in a row. I can't have her dying of starvation so I'm giving you one last chance. The conditions are these: I drop her at your rented flat each weekday morning until she's due to return to school. She stays with you there until I pick her up when I've finished work. You do not leave the flat for any reason. I've got her a new mobile phone and I will call her on it from time to time. If she doesn't answer, I collect her. Skye has agreed to this arrangement. You agree to it too or there's no deal. I will force feed her on a drip if necessary. Call me back in the morning to discuss further.

'Since you asked me a personal question, let me ask you one.'

'Yes, mummy has a boyfriend. Please don't be jealous.'

He had to suppress the urge to guffaw. 'OK, honey. I'll try. But it won't be easy.'

'You're lying, I can tell. You don't care if she has a boyfriend, and I can't blame you. She's a big meanie.'

'That's not fair. I know she can be…stubborn, but she's

a great mum to you and I won't hear otherwise. Now, have you really got a Queen?'

She waltzed back to her seat, handed Jack the requested card and picked up another from the deck. It was the last card and she laid down her four-of-a-kind with a flourish. 'Up for another game?'

———

AS MUCH AS Skye loved her father, there were only so many board games you could play until cabin fever took hold. With a week to go before Jack's flight home, Sarah Lisbon's position shifted again. Skye's constant, whiny nagging had become unbearable and her mother capitulated.

True to form, there was a caveat. They were now allowed outside Jack's Airbnb in Lordship Lane, East Dulwich, but wherever they went, Sarah, like Mary's little lamb, was sure to go. So now, sitting at the same McDonald's where Elrod Smart was working the counter, turning his head away when Jack cast glances in his direction, Sarah occupied a seat just a few yards away from Jack and Skye.

'Are you finding this a little…disturbing?' Jack said to Skye, gesturing with his head towards Sarah, who was stuffing her mouth full of fries. 'I've been on stake-outs, and it's poor form to be in plain sight like that.'

'Yes. It is kind of embarrassing, but what can I say? Mum's mum.'

Yes, it was embarrassing, cringey embarrassing. Jack couldn't care less. He was with his daughter, and that was all that mattered.

Chapter Thirty-Four

'JUST A COPY of *The Daily Mail*, thank you. Oh, and a packet of spearmint gum.' Jack paid for the newspaper with the last of his UK coins. 'For when my ears pop.' He smiled inanely at the young girl behind the counter, grabbed the handle of his carry-on bag and headed for the Qantas Lounge. He scanned the ever-changing notice boards as he went. His flight to Brisbane via Singapore was delayed by twenty minutes. Nothing to stress about. Inside the private area, he ordered a double espresso and a toasted cheese and tomato sandwich and scouted out a soft chair to relax in while he waited to board the jumbo. He was going to miss Skye like crazy, but, if he was going to be totally honest with himself, he'd had enough of the Old Dart. Too many people, too much activity, too many enemies. Bring on the lazy, safe tropics.

He got comfortable in the leather recliner, flicked open the newspaper. The lead story started on the front page and continued on page five. Jack shook his head in disbelief as he read the details. A raid on McNair's house in East

Kilbride yesterday unearthed a frightening list. On it were the names of thirty prominent people – politicians, sports and music stars – targeted for future abductions. Skye had been a trial run. Thankfully, a failure. The article praised Police Scotland for their professionalism in catching the criminals before they were able to go on a kidnapping spree. A journalist from the paper had tried to contact Jack via Pedersen yesterday, but the DCI told him to bugger off. It didn't stop the reporter from inventing colourful details, including getting an artist from their graphics department to recreate the raid in the form of a snazzy diagram. Jack scratched his chin appreciatively – it was pretty close to reality. The answer to the accurate portrayal was on page five. An "anonymous" source had provided the details. Which one of the ARV officers could that have been, Jack wondered.

Jack stretched his legs out in front of him. The recliner was the most comfortable chair he'd ever sat in. He made a mental note to take a couple of pictures on his phone and look for something similar when he got home. He sipped his coffee before tackling the last paragraph of the article.

Before he could read it, his phone vibrated. Unknown number. Didn't matter, he was out of harm's way in the confines of the airport. Spurred by a copper's curiosity he answered. 'Jack Lisbon, wot?'

'You think you've gotten away with it, don't you?' A shaky female voice.

'Excuse me, who is this?' Jack already knew the answer.

'It's Alicia Rafter.'

'I can understand your anger.' Jack feigned politeness with a casual laugh. 'I apologise for the subterfuge with my mate pretending to be a private investigator 'n all. We simply wanted to eliminate you from our enquiries.'

'Don't play stupid, dickhead,' she hissed. 'I'm onto you. You killed my father and I'm going to make you pay. I don't care how long it takes, or what I have to do to have you put away.'

'Aren't you happy an innocent girl was rescued?'

'I feel sorry for her, having a criminal scumbag for a father.'

Jack looked around to make sure no one was listening. 'I strongly advise you to seek psychological help, madam.'

'Don't call me madam and don't you dare tell me what to do, you murderer!' she thundered.

'Be very careful how you choose your words. I'm recording this call.'

'You're bluffing.' She sounded unsure. 'You wouldn't risk it.'

'I'll be handing the audio over to the Met. They can deal with you as they see fit. I'm guessing a minor harassment charge.' He lowered his tone a fraction. 'I'd hate to see you declared mentally unstable and struck off the dentists' register.'

'Fuck you!'

'Good-bye, Alicia.' Jack ended the call.

Back to the paper. The article concluded with a statement from the police that the newly discovered list would lead to a string of extra charges being laid, including conspiracy to kidnap and defraud. Brilliant.

No doubt the story would capture the country's imagination for a while until the next big thing, Jack mused. He'd follow developments closely from Australia, do everything he could to make sure McNair and his stooges spent the majority of their natural lives behind bars.

After ordering a second coffee, Jack thought it might be nice to talk to a friend, to lift his mood before take-off.

There was an ulterior motive – he wanted to find out if she had any feelings for him. He sucked in a deep breath and made the call on her work number. 'DC Taylor speaking.' A sleepy, croaky voice.

'It's me. What time is it there?'

'A quarter to six in the bloody morning. Don't you normally check before you call?'

'Correct, I do. But sometimes it's fun to do things on the spur of the moment, don't you agree?'

'Not when it's still pitch dark here it isn't.' Jack heard a soft rustling sound. 'What do you want, Jack? The bad guys are in jail, aren't they?'

'Yep.' He wasn't sure how to frame the next part. Perhaps make a wee joke out of it. 'I was just calling for a chat before my flight. I'll be home soon.'

'Yay,' she said in a sluggish voice that sounded anything but celebratory. 'I'll organise one of those water-canon receptions at Yorkville airport, shall I?'

'No need for that. Hey, you'll never guess what my cheeky daughter told me.'

'Try me.'

'She said my ex reckons you and I are…ah…an item.'

The sound of things banging.

'Did you hear me?' said Jack.

'No, I was trying to coax a giant spider out the window. Can you repeat it?'

His courage deserted him. *Forget it, Lisbon.* 'Nothing important, Claudia. Go back to bed. Sorry to disturb you.'

'Don't stress about it. I was intending on going for a run anyway. I'm aspiring to reach your level of fitness.'

'Right. I'll see you then.'

'Sure. I'll be glad to see you back on deck. I've really missed you.'

'You have?'

'Yeah.'

'In a professional sense?' Shit. *Should he have even said it?*

'Mostly, but not exclusively. See you, Jack.' She ended the call.

As a voice came over a loudspeaker asking passengers on Flight QF2 to make their way to the boarding gate, Jack gave a little fist pump. *Mostly* was a good start.

Next in the Fighting Detective Series

vinci-books.com/dropshot

The glamorous world of professional tennis collides with the gritty underbelly of crime. Detective Jack Lisbon finds himself entangled in a perplexing murder case when a tennis prodigy is discovered dead in a seedy hotel room.

Keep turning the pages for a free preview…

A free prequel novella...

vinci-books.com/takedown-free

Get the explosive prequel to The Fighting Detective series, absolutely free.

Drop Shot: Chapter One

THE LATE AFTERNOON sun shimmered like an incandescent disc against a vast lapis canvas. It beat down with a ferocity to match the efforts of the two players, who sizzled tennis balls across the net while the spectators in the stands struggled to raise a cold drink to their lips. The punishing heat, even with nightfall less than half an hour away, helped to create patches of sweat that bloomed on the athletes' clothing. The men had needed to change their sopping shirts and socks at the end of the first set. As a man who grew up in the cooler climes of Great Britain, ex-pat Detective Sergeant Jack Lisbon of the Queensland Police Service was able to sympathise with them. The conditions on court were almost unbearable.

He tugged the brim of his baseball cap lower over his eyes as the sun invaded his line of sight. Jack had almost declined the invitation to attend the tournament, but for a sports fan the opportunity to see a top-ten ranked player in action proved irresistible. Worth putting up with a few hours of outdoor discomfort. His boss, Inspector Joe Batista, had been comped two tickets for him and his wife but, thankfully, they had other plans. The chief passed them on to Jack who gleefully accepted the gift.

As the serving player double faulted and the crowd groaned in sympathy, Jack sensed his partner Detective Constable Claudia Taylor leaning across and into him. It was counterintuitive to back off; her presence usually demanded closer proximity. But the heat was too intense to be rubbing up to another human being, no matter how much you were attracted to them.

The next point was over in a flash. From the left-hand side of the court, the favourite returned serve with a flick of the wrist, the ball scorching past his opponent's desperate outstretched racquet. A ball-boy arched his back to avoid being tagged by the little green missile, which thundered into an advertising sign. The crowd clapped in appreciation of the master's supreme skill. The enthusiasm behind the applause had waned over the course of the match, which, in Jack's opinion, was the most one-sided contest he'd seen since Manny Pacquiao knocked the bejesus out of Ricky Hatton in 2009. Still, the punters had paid their entrance fees and would watch the slaughter to the bitter end. The slack-jawed umpire drawled out the call. *Game McAdam. He leads five games to love, second set.* The players crossed paths at the net post as they headed for their seats before changing ends. The challenger's head hung low and his feet dragged, the champion bouncing and grinning from ear to ear. The world number ten, cocky local lad Roderick McAdam prone to volatile temper tantrums, had only dropped two points in the match. Win the next game – on his own serve – and the match was his. He was in a class of his own against the poor opponent, Sean Depp, a non-ranked player from Perth.

'A closed-roof stadium with air-conditioning is what's

required for this climate,' bemoaned Jack. He used the sleeve of his already drenched t-shirt to mop up droplets of perspiration from the skin between his nose and upper lip. A wasted effort, since new sweat beaded to replace that which had been wiped away. 'This damn humidity's giving me a headache.' He grabbed a bottle of purple Powerade from under his flip-down plastic seat and guzzled the contents like his life depended on it. 'This is the bleedin' tropics. You'd think they'd schedule play for night time, innit?'

'And you'd think a smart bloke like you would know plain old water is better for quenching your thirst than that gimmicky rubbish.'

'Each to their own, Claudia.' He pointed at tiny writing on the label. 'This stuff's got extra vitamins and minerals in it. Replenishes lost energy.'

'Whatever,' she chuckled.

'Give me some ice, will ya.'

Taylor pulled a blue foam cooler box out from under her seat and opened the lid. Jack reached in and took out a handful of ice cubes, rubbed them over his face and dropped a couple of them down the back of his neck and the front of his shirt. He closed his eyes tight as the cubes worked their cooling magic.

Taylor observed his antics goggle-eyed. 'If it's too much for you, just say the word. We can go somewhere else and watch it on TV. From the inside of a pub.'

'Don't be daft.' He waved his hand around. 'Look at all the people here enduring it. Lots of them are old-age pensioners. If they can handle it, so can I.'

Jack took the opportunity of the short break to flick through a program he'd purchased. The tournament, The Pilmer Challenge, was the brainchild of local billionaire sugar magnate Clyde Pilmer. It was a bizarre competition, billed as the tennis equivalent of the old boxing tents, where unknowns could slug it out with travelling professional boxers for a bag full of money. In this case, Pilmer was offering a winner-take-all first prize of five million dollars, dwarfing the money up for grabs at the Australian Open, due to start in two weeks. Only sixteen players – unranked amateurs hand-picked by Pilmer from club competitions around the nation – were admitted to the tournament, with the notable exception of local boy Roderick McAdam, at just 19 years-old already number 10 in the world. McAdam could claim the coveted number one spot in two weeks' time by winning the Australian Open, with the proviso that a couple of top seeds crashed out early. Pilmer had paid all the competitors' travel and accommodation expenses – including for McAdam, the only one who could actually pay his own way. Unheard-of bonus incentives were the bait for the journeymen: $500,000 to take a set off McAdam and $250,000 just to break his serve. McAdam was the lion, the challengers – the lambs to the slaughter.

Jack folded the program and put it back in his pocket. With only four players left in the tournament, so far Pilmer hadn't had to shell out a penny in prize money. In fact, he was raking in the dollars from pay TV deals he'd made with the world's biggest broadcasters. The event was so bizarre it had generated massive interest. Jack understood why. It was like the macabre enjoyment people get from watching a car crash. In any case, it was shaping up as a huge payday for McAdam with the pretenders – barring a miracle – destined to go home empty-handed apart from their fifteen minutes of fame.

The umpire gave a time warning, as the players took every second of their allotted break to sit under broad umbrellas and pour liquids into their dehydrating bodies.

Depp's head disappeared into a water-soaked towel, while McAdam pulled a brand new racquet out of a bag, peeled off the plastic cover and tapped the strings against the palm of his hand. Jack thought it was ridiculous the bloke needed a new weapon to dispatch his teetering foe – he could almost deliver the final knock-out with a ping pong paddle. Young Depp probably couldn't afford to use more than one racquet per match. The umpire called the men back out onto the court in his flat-voweled Aussie drawl.

Jack glanced at his watch. 6:54pm. The sun had just dipped under the horizon, but it would still be light for another hour or so. This was the last match scheduled for the day, and thank God for that. He prayed McAdam would quickly and humanely finish off his victim so everyone could go home. Four aces in a row would be good. He felt the urge to have a wager with Taylor.

'I reckon Depp won't lay a racquet on the ball,' said Jack, waving a twenty-dollar bill in her face. 'And if he does, it's straight into the net or out.'

'Last of the big-time gamblers, huh? OK. You're on, Lisbon. I reckon he can at least win a point.'

Quiet please, said the umpire from his little crow's nest. The crowd of a thousand or so spectators at the Yorkville Tennis Centre went silent as one, waiting to see the end to the challenger's abject humiliation in front of a global audience of millions.

Jack focused his eyes on the receiver. He'd been watching Depp more than McAdam for the majority of the match. Most would be looking at McAdam as he prepared to serve, Jack knew that, but this public thrashing interested Jack much more as a psychological study of the inevitable loser.

Depp had started the first game of the match with poise,

immediately wrangling two points off McAdam's opening service game to be up 0–30. Spectators oohed and aahed, anticipating a boilover and the no-name player scoring a massive prize.

But it wasn't to be. Staring at the prospect of a $250,000 payday, Depp either choked or McAdam decided to stop toying with his prey and step on his opponent's throat. McAdam reeled in the points. Bang, bang, bang, game. And with that, Depp was a lame duck with every bit of confidence gone.

A quick glance to the left confirmed that McAdam had finished his five-bounce settling routine. Then Jack shifted his gaze back to Depp. For the first time in the short and brutal match, there was a glimmer of something positive in the unranked player's expression, a spark of determination. Jaw set firmly, feet planted wide, body low and swaying. The guy had made up his mind – he was utterly destroyed but he'd go out swinging. In his peripherals Jack observed the high ball toss, the blur of the racquet as McAdam bent his back and swung up to meet the ball. The *ping* of the ball connecting with the fresh strings of the new implement was like a gunshot. Depp took a wild swing as the ball homed in on his racquet's sweet spot and the ball whistled back low over the net well out of the reach of McAdam, rooted to the spot.

0–15.

A repeat of the oohs and aahs from the first game of the first set. Was there something special about to happen?

Jack heard a soft cough to his left. Taylor, grinning, held out her hand and Jack dropped a twenty note in her palm. She winked a *thank you* and they both looked back to the court.

McAdam flicked his fingers at a ball boy standing

ramrod straight behind the baseline. The kid understood the signal and bounced a ball to the server. McAdam swatted the ball away contemptuously and nodded for another. This one seemed to be to his liking. He took a deep breath and again went through his routine. Five bounces, a flick of sweat from his brow. Jack again fixed his attention on the receiver. More motion in his sway, Depp stood in line with the doubles lane. Whack. Depp had guessed wrong. The ball flew down the centre of the court like a rocket, landing just inside the service box. Depp didn't even try to reach this one.

15–15.

The crowd seemed to lose its hope like a balloon leaking air. The next two points came in the form of a pair of blistering aces.

40–15 and match point. The end would surely come with the next serve. McAdam had found his groove again. Still, Jack observed the receiver.

Fault, called the chair umpire.

Depp bounced up and down on his toes again. Jack wasn't sure, but he thought he detected a snarl on the challenger's face, as if he was saying to McAdam, *Bring it, arsehole!*

The second serve dipped over the net with a wicked curl, but swung wide, landing six inches outside the service line. *Double fault*. 40–30. Still match point. This time Jack switched his gaze to McAdam. What was going on?

The champion bounced the ball ten times instead of the trademark five, tossed the ball high, but then backed away at the last second, waving a hand in front of his face. 'These bloody flies!' he yelled. The crowd chuckled. After a shrug of the shoulders and a wipe of his face with a tiny towel tucked in the back of his shorts, he sent down another thunderbolt. Jack's eyes darted to the other side of the net. The ball was an Exocet missile, all Depp could do was desperately block it with the racquet held firmly in front of his face, eyes shut tight. The ball ricocheted off the strings, lobbed high into the air, and then gently plopped over McAdam's head after he'd followed through on his serve all the way to the net. The ball landed a foot inside the line.

Deuce.

Now the crowd was wriggling like one big agitated mass of worms. The champ had not had to face a score like this in the first two elimination matches. Spectators were gibbering so loudly the ump had to call for silence again.

Fault! The first serve was way long, landing almost at Depp's feet.

Jack wondered what was going through McAdam's brain.

Double fault! This one sailed into the net, halfway up.

Advantage Depp.

The crowd were on their feet, whistling, stomping and cheering. McAdam bent double, racquet planted handle-end onto the blue surface of the Rebound Ace court, hands on the racquet head and chin resting on the back of his hands. He held the pose for twenty seconds before straightening. At the other end, Depp was hopping up and down like he was walking on a bed of hot coals.

McAdam took a couple of deep breaths, performed the standard routine. The serve took Depp by surprise – half strength and with a vicious swing to the left. Depp scrambled, returned with a weak sliced backhand that clipped the top of the net before landing half-way down the court, sitting up nicely for McAdam to destroy any way he chose. McAdam uncoiled his body and let rip with a scorching forehand cross-court passing shot.

Deuce, said the umpire.

A roar went up from the crowd. Jack and Taylor were screaming too, but not in appreciation of McAdam's skill. The ball was clearly out, everyone could see it – except for the lineswoman and the chair umpire. The game – and $250,000 – was rightfully Depp's.

Jack turned to Taylor. 'Did you see that? Six inches out!'

Taylor didn't reply as she screwed up her eyes, focussing on the reaction of the wronged player. Jack watched Depp, too. The man wasn't going to take this travesty of justice lying down. Instead of approaching the umpire to complain, Depp threw his racquet to one side, marched to the net, clasped both hands together imploringly. The crowd went silent, eager to hear the exchange.

'What the hell are you playing at?' said Depp. Courtside microphones picked up the chat and delivered it to the spectators over loudspeakers.

'I'm playing by the rules.' McAdam wore an affronted expression. 'Now, go back and prepare to receive so I can finish you off.'

'C'mon, Rod, I won the game. Don't do this, mate!' Depp was a lightly built man who looked far from intimidating, but one could imagine smoke pouring from his ears.

'Do what?' McAdam stared at his fingernails.

'Be a man and concede the point to me. Everyone saw the ball was a mile out.' Depp looked up at the mass of people in the stand opposite the umpire, cupped his hands to his mouth. 'Didn't you?' he hollered.

'YES!' came the almost unanimous reply.

McAdam shook his head. 'Mate, I didn't see it. I have to trust the officials, there's no challenge procedure in place, no hawk-eye technology. We all knew that when we signed up.' He shrugged. 'The officials are paid good money to make the calls, not me.'

The remark about the money seemed a deliberate provocation. Depp had just been deprived of the equivalent of a lottery win to your average Joe. A life-changing event for a man who was no more than a very good pennant-level tennis player.

'You're a dirty cheat, McAdam. An arrogant son of a bitch!' He pointed an accusing forefinger at the trembling lineswoman, 'You!', and then at the chair umpire, who's face was granite-calm despite the unfolding melodrama... 'and you! You two are a fucking disgrace. Paid off by Pilmer to make sure that bastard wins everything!'

A large section of the crowd cheered approvingly. The world number ten enjoyed a reputation as one of the tennis tour's bad boys, a modern-day John McEnroe for whom winning meant everything. McAdam decided to rub salt into the wound. 'Nobody cares about your opinion, whatever your name is.'

The same section of the audience that cheered Depp now booed McAdam, who had far fewer fans in the stands now that he'd decided to play hardball with the underdog. But he wasn't about to change tack to placate his detractors, no matter how loud and numerous. 'You're cooked, son. I won the point fair and square. But hang in there, it's back to deuce. You'll just have to try harder to earn that cash for breaking my serve. How much was it again? Oh yeah, a quarter of a million dollars.' McAdam tilted his head back and roared with laughter.

In the blink of an eye, Depp had jumped the net and was right up in McAdam's grill. Their heated conversation was white-noise, each screaming obscenities at the other, noses inches apart. Within fifteen seconds, four men in black shirts had raced onto the court, two quickly restrained Depp as he cocked his right arm ready to throw a punch. They pulled him away as the two other goons stood like bodyguards in front of the millionaire sports star, arms folded across their chests.

'Holy hell,' said Taylor. 'If this weird-arse tournament on its own doesn't get Yorkville on the world map, that scuffle certainly will.' She pointed at the prostrate figure of Depp the aggressor, restrained by two bald gorillas from Pilmer's security team.

'You're not wrong,' Jack laughed. 'This is better than pro wrestling. But I feel sorry for the lad.'

'Robbed blind, I'd say. But we've certainly got our money's worth.' Taylor held her phone aloft, as did a large percentage of the crowd. It reminded Jack of fans at rock concerts, more concerned with getting a memento than actually enjoying the show.

Jack slugged more Powerade, gestured towards Taylor's mobile. 'You getting a video for Facebook?'

'No. Evidence. In case it gets really nasty and someone gets hurt.'

Jack had to call bullshit on that one. 'Rubbish. There's TV cameras everywhere getting it all on tape. The hired muscle seem to have it under control.'

'Actually, you *were* right,' she grinned, caught out on her little fib. 'Almost. It's for Instagram. Facebook is so yesterday.'

'Is it now?' Jack's relationship with social media was like the one he had with his ex-wife. Infrequent and troublesome.

All eyes and ears were fixated on the running scrum at the eastern end of centre court. The security detail escorted a wriggling and screaming Depp off centre stage, through a dark tunnel and, presumably, into the dressing room. Just before disappearing, Depp managed to turn around and offer a parting word, clearly audible to everyone. 'You're fucked, McAdam!' He tried to yell out something else but one of the security men wrapped a hand around Depp's mouth and muffled the words.

The umpire waited for the excited crowd to pipe down, which took a good five minutes. Once he'd obviously decided full silence was not returning, he ploughed on through the hubbub, thanked all the on-court officials, players and ball boys and girls, and especially the sponsor, Pilmer Enterprises. All the while, McAdam sat motionless in his plastic chair, head covered by a lime-green towel, as his coach massaged his shoulders.

Pilmer would be rubbing his hands with glee, thought Jack. Outstanding publicity. A packed auditorium and off-the-charts TV ratings would be guaranteed for tomorrow's final against…Jack had to consult the program again…a Tasmanian left-hander called Hugh Marshall.

A reporter from a major network tried to interview McAdam. She only got two questions into it before she had to abandon the attempt. The aggravated crowd's renewed jeering was too much. Microphone by her side, she headed for the safety of the exit.

Bag slung over his shoulder, McAdam smiled and waved triumphantly even as the spectators saw him off with another barrage of whistles, boos and insults under a shower of food and drink containers.

In the blink of an eye, Australia's misunderstood golden boy had become its most hated athlete.

Drop Shot: Chapter Two

'DID you enjoy the tennis last night, DS Lisbon?' asked Yorkville Police Station's lanky boss, Inspector Joe Batista. 'I heard there was a huge drama at the end of the match.'

Jack took a sip of his take-away double-espresso, set the paper cup back on his desk and started rolling up his shirt-sleeves. 'That's an understatement, guv. I've never seen anything like it. You don't happen to have any tickets for the final tonight, do you?' The final, as opposed to the daytime preliminary matches, was scheduled for 8:00pm, under lights. On his drive in to work Jack heard over the radio that McAdam had demanded the organisers switch the time or else he'd walk and the event wouldn't go any further. Despite three easy victories – the last one via Depp's disqualification for unsportsmanlike behaviour – he claimed his body was beginning to wilt in the lead up to the Australian Open, something he couldn't tolerate further despite the enormous prize money on offer. He had the world number one ranking in his sights, after all.

The chief shook his head. 'Sadly, no, DS Lisbon. But

why would you want to watch a repeat of that fiasco? To be honest, the whole concept doesn't sit right with me. It's like a public execution.'

'I don't know,' said Taylor hopefully. 'With the entire country behind him, the Tassie kid might actually have a chance. He slaughtered his three opponents on the other side of the draw.'

Jack tapped a couple of keys on his work computer to log in. 'And who were they, Claudia? Worthy adversaries or third-rate wannabes like poor old Sean Depp.'

She raised her shoulders in a mini shrug. 'I don't know.'

'I'll tell you in a minute.' Jack picked up a copy of *The Yorkville Times*, licked his finger and flicked to the sports section. 'Looks like Pilmer's been sourcing his victims from far and wide. Facing off against McAdam in the final is Hugh Marshall. Top-ranked amateur in Tasmania.' He leaned back in his swivel chair and cracked a couple of knuckles before resuming his perusal of the paper. His hands ached slightly from an overly enthusiastic session with the heavy bag after his morning jog. 'And Claudia, you're dead right. Marshall flogged the three blokes on the other side of the draw as easily as McAdam beat his opponents. He's booted out, lemme see, Charles Jalin from Melbourne, Quinn Chapman from Sydney and Craig Young from Adelaide. Score lines of 6–0, 6–0, same as McAdam.'

'Doesn't mean this Marshall has a hope against McAdam, though,' said Taylor. 'The difference in ability is like chalk and cheese.'

'True.' Jack nodded. 'Plus there's the fact McAdam is a full-time pro while the other blokes are part-timers.' He took another sip of coffee. 'But even so, it looks like whoever organised the draw wanted the strongest of the also-rans safe from McAdam so the amateur could at least have a chance in the final. Might even get that $250,000 Depp missed out on.'

'Let's see how much of a chance this guy is.' Taylor clicked on her mouse, adjusted her glasses and peered intently at the screen. Jack could see the list of search engine results reflected in Taylor's glasses. She clicked the second link in the list. 'It says here Marshall was a hot prospect as a junior, but he was hit by tragedy and dropped out of the tennis scene for a number of years.'

'What happened?' said Constable Ben Wilson from his desk on the other side of the office. 'The story's ringing bells.'

'Oh my God!' cried Taylor.

'What?' Wilson again.

'His mother and father were murdered in their beds seven years ago. Poor kid.' She took a sip of tea before fixing her attention back on the computer. 'The culprit was never caught. Marshall himself was a suspect at the beginning.'

'Incredible.' Jack sat up straight.

'Hang on, here's a link to an interview he gave after he was asked to play in the Pilmer Challenge. Marshall was seventeen when his mum and dad were killed. He had a complete mental breakdown. Hobart detectives had him under a microscope for two years before they finally cut him loose as a suspect. There was incriminating DNA evidence at the scene, but there was also other DNA that couldn't be identified. Plus it was impossible to find a motive; the parents died penniless and there was no inheritance. After the murder he moved in with an auntie. Four years of therapy and serious medication. One day he decided enough was enough, applied for university and earned himself a science degree. He's currently working as a marine biologist in Hobart, Tasmania.'

'Anything more about the murder investigation?' said Jack eagerly.

'Not in this article. The questions in the second half of the piece are about him rebuilding his life.' Her lips moved as she read in silence. Then she concluded, 'He went back to tennis to keep fit, the early natural talent returned and he soared to the top of the amateur ranks in Tasmania.'

Batista coughed into his fist. 'Ah, as much as I find this whole soap opera fascinating, don't we have some important police work to do?'

Taylor removed her reading glasses, tied her dark hair back with a yellow scrunchie and smiled at the chief. 'Indeed we have, sir. A big drugs case, as it happens.'

'Operation Antarctic Freeze,' said Batista. 'It's up before the magistrate today, right?'

'Correct,' Taylor nodded. 'Jack and I have to give evidence and Constable Wilson here's assisting. We're about to put our lippy on and head over to the courthouse in…' she glanced at her watch… 'two minutes.'

'Good luck with the testimony,' Batista smiled encouragingly. 'I understand you've drawn Nunez as the magistrate. She's a hard nut to crack when it comes to punishing street crime.' The chief stroked his wedge of a chin.

Grab your copy…
vinci-books.com/dropshot

About the Author

Blair Denholm is a born-and-bred Australian crime fiction writer whose previous jobs have been as varied as translator, debt collector, technology researcher, banking and insurance consultant, and even car-wash attendant. Over the years he has lived and worked in New York, Moscow, Munich, Abu Dhabi and Australia. His life-long love of sports is reflected in the plots of The Fighting Detective series.

Denholm's flagship series, The Fighting Detective, stars ex-boxer Detective Sergeant Jack Lisbon and is set in the steamy tropics of North Queensland, Australia. The series features heavy doses of noir crime with a vigilante justice twist. So far there are eight novels and one prequel novella in the series, with more in the pipeline.

Denholm's debut novel, *SOLD*, is the first in a noir trilogy featuring the detestable yet lovable one-man wrecking ball Gary Braswell. The book was long-listed for movie adaptation by Screen Queensland in 2019. The other books in this series are *Sold to the Devil* and *Sold Dirt Cheap*.

Denholm has also written two thriller novels set in Russia. Captain Viktor Voloshin is a hard-boiled investigator who has to fight the establishment in order for justice to be served in his own special way. The first in this series, *Revolution Day*, was published in 2021, with the follow-up, *The Defector*, released in 2024. One more book will round off this series.

In 2024, Denholm signed on with UK-based publisher Vinci Books.

Blair Denholm grew up in suburban Brisbane, Queensland. After two lengthy stints in Tasmania, he now resides in the relatively cooler climes of the Southern Downs region of Queensland with his partner, Sandra, and faithful dog, Bruno.

Acknowledgments

When I wrote a novella about a corrupt cop given a chance at redemption, I never thought it would evolve into the series that it is, and the series that it will be. Now at novel number four, I can't see an end to the adventures of Detective Jack Lisbon. And to get this far, you need a lot of help. Here's a shout out to: Sandra my love, Bruno my body guard, proofreaders Don Hawthorne and Jiver Freecloud, my supportive American crime writer friends, in particular Gary McAvoy. Thank you all!

www.ingramcontent.com/pod-product-compliance
Ingram Content Group UK Ltd.
Pitfield, Milton Keynes, MK11 3LW, UK
UKHW040229220126
467235UK00004B/56